Lady with an Alien

Lady with an Alien

with an Alien

An Encounter with Leonardo da Vinci

MIKE RESNICK

WATSON-GUPTILL PUBLICATIONS/NEW YORK

Series Editor: Jacqueline Ching
Editor: Laaren Brown
Production Manager: Hector Campbell
Book Design: Jennifer Browne

First published in 2005 in the United States by Watson-Guptill Publications,
a division of VNU Business Media, Inc.,
770 Broadway, New York, NY 10003
www.wgpub.com

Front cover: Leonardo da Vinci, *Lady with an Ermine*, ca. 1490, Czartorysky Museum,
Krakow, Poland. Photo credit: Erich-Lessing/Art Resource, NY. Back cover: Leonardo da
Vinci, by anonymous. Uffizi, Florence, Italy. Photo credit: Scala/Art Resource, NY.
Chapter art from *Banners, Ribbons & Scrolls: An Archive for Artists and Designers*, edited by
Carol Belanger Grafton, Dover Publications, Inc.

Library of Congress Cataloging-in-Publication Data
Resnick, Michael D.
Lady with an alien : an encounter with Leonardo da Vinci / by Mike Resnick.
p. cm.—(Art encounters)
Summary: A young boy, Mario Ravelli, develops a unique relationship with
the great painter and inventor, Leonardo da Vinci, particularly because Mario
is a time traveler from the year 2523 A.D.
ISBN 0-8230-0323-X
International Paperback ISBN 0-8230-0419-8
1. Leonardo, da Vinci, 1452-1519—Juvenile fiction. [1. Leonardo, da Vinci, 1452-1519—
Fiction. 2. Artists—Fiction. 3. Time travel—Fiction.] I. Title. II. Series.
PZ7.R31634Lad 2005 [Fic]—dc22 2005011920

This book was set in Stempel Garamond.

Printed in the U.S.A.
First printing, 2005
1 2 3 4 5 6 7 8 9 / 12 11 10 09 08 07 06 05

To Carol, as always,
and to Jackie Ching

Contents

Preface

It is said of Leonardo da Vinci that one day he awoke from his slumber, opened his eyes, and found that the rest of the world was still asleep.

As an illegitimate child he was not permitted to learn Latin or Greek, the languages of art and scholarship in the fifteenth century. He was not permitted to enter the legal or medical professions. Many doors were closed to him—so he simply invented new doors.

He became, along with Michelangelo and Rafael, one of the three most heralded painters of his era and produced the single most famous painting in history: the *Mona Lisa*. Even today, almost five hundred years after his death, he is considered among the half-dozen greatest artists Western civilization has produced.

And yet, despite the esteem in which his art is held, Leonardo was much more than simply a painter.

His extensive notebooks show that he had a profound knowledge of human anatomy, at least partially obtained from dissecting corpses. His knowledge of birds and some domestic animals was almost as great.

He first came to the attention of Ludovico Sforza, who was his patron at the time this story takes place, when he designed movable bridges for Sforza's army, which were inconceivable before Leonardo invented them.

He designed a working parachute and terrible war engines of destruction. (The British army, as an experiment, built one based on Leonardo's drawings some 465 years after the fact, and it actually worked.) He had planned to create an enormous bronze horse, the biggest ever seen, and produced a clay model; but then Sforza decided to use the bronze for cannons instead, and the project was never completed.

And until the day he died, he tried to design a method by which humans could fly. He never did, of course, but some of his sketches show that he grasped the principles of keeping gliders aloft.

And, oh yes, he had a lovely singing voice, danced with the grace of a cat, and could play a number of musical instruments.

He lived in the Renaissance; and when people speak of a "Renaissance man," they mean, whether they know it or not, Leonardo, who exemplifies all that the term implies. If he had a flaw, it is the number of unfinished projects he left behind. So many wildly different things captured his interest that he had a difficult time concentrating on a single project for any length of time. (How difficult? Michelangelo painted the entire ceiling of the Sistine Chapel in less time than it took Leonardo to paint the *Mona Lisa*.)

This book concerns the creation of what Isabella d'Este, one of the greatest women patrons and collectors of all time, called "the first modern painting in history," the painting known as *Lady with an Ermine*.

Why did I choose it? Because Leonardo was a naturalistic painter, not an impressionist. He painted what he saw—and that little animal simply doesn't look like an ermine to me.

I am a science fiction writer by trade, and I felt science fiction was the perfect vehicle to mix fact with imagination and create an answer to the mystery of *Lady with an Ermine*.

And it was fun to visit with Leonardo while I was writing this.

Prospero

I hate that cat, thought Leonardo irritably.

The cat, secure on its owner's lap, looked up at the artist and gave him a smug feline grin.

"He moved again," said Leonardo. "Please try to hold him still. He keeps changing the way the cloth on your sleeve lays."

"He is my sweetheart, aren't you, Prospero?" said the young woman, running her long slender fingers down the cat's back. The animal stretched and purred.

I thought my patron was your sweetheart, thought Leonardo. *If he isn't, why have I wasted an entire year with this portrait?*

Aloud he said, "Are you absolutely sure you want Prospero in the painting? There is still time to eliminate him."

"I won't hear of it!" snapped the young woman. "Ludovico ordered you to paint me. Now paint!"

Ludovico Sforza is the Regent of Milan, and I have known him longer than you, thought Leonardo. *In fact, he has owed me money longer than he has known you, which is why I am wasting my time with this portrait when so many fascinating things beckon.*

But of course he did not say these things aloud. One does not complain about the duke's tight-fistedness to his mistress, even when he is one's patron and has been begging one to create enormous engines of war and destruction for him. She would run right to Sforza and relate what Leonardo said, and sooner or later even Sforza would figure out that it was easier and certainly less expensive to turn Leonardo over to the Inquisition than to pay him.

But this empty-headed girl and her cat were eating into his time, and he resented it. Every time that cat moved it cost the meticulous Leonardo another hour's work, and that was an hour he couldn't spend on his notebooks or his experiments. He was on the brink of creating a machine that could fly; he felt it in his bones—three, four, at the most five uninterrupted nights and he'd have it.

But how could he concentrate when there were the almost daily sessions with Cecilia Gallerani, who, he noted, had just lost her pose again while petting the cat? And then there were the messages from Sforza himself: Is it done? Is it progressing? How soon will it be done? *Why* isn't it done?

Leonardo knew the real reason for Sforza's anxiety. *Il Moro*—"the Moor," as the Regent was known—wanted those war machines. But while he was fearless in battle, he lacked the courage to tell Cecilia that the machines were more important to him than the completion of her portrait. So he nagged.

Incessantly.

"Let us stop for the day," said Leonardo. "I am losing my light."

"It's midafternoon," replied Cecilia. "You will have light enough for two more hours at least."

Leonardo sighed. He could fabricate a story about the lengthening of the shadows, but she'd see right through it as easily as he could see through any shadows.

"As you wish," he said.

But suddenly Prospero jumped out of her arms and onto the floor.

"He needs to . . ." began Cecilia, as the cat walked to the door.

"Yes, I know," said Leonardo. He turned to Cecilia's maid, who had been standing patiently in a corner. "Please let him out."

The maid opened the door, and the cat shot out into the street. The first time that had happened Leonardo had hoped it was the last any of them would ever see of the cat, but the feline never strayed more than a few feet from the door.

Cecilia got to her feet. "I suppose we can stop for today," she said. "The only reason I wanted to continue working was because Ludovico is going to Naples tomorrow morning and I will be going with him. So you won't be able to work on my portrait for almost three weeks."

"I am crestfallen," said Leonardo. And silently he added, *Thank you, God.*

"Try not to be too bored while I am gone," said Cecilia.

"It will be an effort, but I shall endeavor not to," promised Leonardo.

"Good-bye then," she said, following her maid out the door.

Leonardo walked to a window and watched as the maid picked up the cat, tucked him under an arm, and stood aside as Cecilia entered the sedan chair that Sforza had supplied. The two burly men who had been stationed by the chair picked it up and began carrying it down the street. Leonardo uttered a sigh of pure relief, walked over to his

pile of notebooks, picked up the top one, opened it, and began studying the drawings he had made the night before.

There *had* to be a way for a man to remain aloft. He was on the
right track, but he was missing something, something that was staring
him right in the face. But what? The arms and torso had to be free to
adjust to turns, the feet had to be kept together and extended out
behind. Birds had hollow bones and men did not, but he had seen
eagles flying off with prey animals clutched in their talons; that had
added considerably to their weight, yet they flew.

He put down the notebook and opened another, one with numerous sketches of the musculature of the human body. Was the answer
here? He turned page after page, frowning, and finally put the book
aside.

He picked up a handful of his notebooks and began paging idly
through them, looking for anything that would spark his imagination,
that would take him that final step. It was an old trick of his: pose the
question to his brain and then distract it with other matters while it
continued to work just beneath the surface until it finally produced
a solution.

Leonardo spent the next two hours reading his books and studying his notes about astronomy, geography, mathematics, philosophy,
religion, and naval warfare. He examined the inventions he had created on paper, changing some details here and there.

He found himself getting hungry. His servant was at a family
funeral in Rome, and he had given his apprentices, who normally
lived with him, a vacation rather than put up with the mess they
created. He decided to cook his own meal. He wasn't sure what he

would make, but it would be something new, something never seen or tasted before. It might even be the source of a new field of study.

He got to his feet, put his notebooks in a neat pile, took another look at Cecilia's portrait, and wondered where his students had left the food. Or indeed if there was any. He realized to his chagrin that he wouldn't know fresh food from spoiled, so he decided to go out to the market to buy something to bring home and cook.

An hour later he returned home, his arms filled with beef, pork, fish, vegetables, and fruits. He had no idea what proportion he would use of each, or even how to cook the food, whether to boil or bake— but that was what made it interesting. A mere dinner would be deadly dull, but an *experiment* he could hardly wait to begin.

He opened the door to his house and carried his purchases into the kitchen, then came back to shut the door. He was laying the food out in orderly piles when he heard a clattering coming from the direction of his studio. He followed the sounds and saw that his pile of notebooks had been knocked to the floor.

The wind? he wondered. *No, of course not. The wind can't blow inside the house.*

It must have been the way he stacked the notebooks. He would have to be more careful in the future. He checked the floor to make sure he hadn't missed any—and saw a tiny footprint. And then another, and another.

"Am I never to be rid of that cat?" he muttered. "Is it not enough that he multiplies the time I must spend on the portrait? Does he now feel free to invade my domain even without his mistress?"

The footprints led behind a chair in the corner of the room.

"All right," said Leonardo, walking over. "Come on out, Prospero. It's time to go home where you belong."

There was no response.

"I am losing my patience, cat," he said more harshly. "Show yourself."

Still nothing.

Leonardo reached out, grabbed the chair, and pulled it toward him.

"I warned you, cat," he said. "Just be grateful that you belong to my patron's mistress and that I can't simply throw you out into the street. Now, where are—?"

Suddenly Leonardo froze, staring in fascination at what he had revealed by moving the chair. It was almost a full minute before he spoke.

"God in heaven," he whispered. "What *are* you?"

Aristotle

The small creature stared up at Leonardo. It had four legs, but as it crouched, the artist could see they were jointed in the wrong places. At first he thought the animal was crippled, but then it took a few graceful steps toward him and he realized that it was built that way.

Its eyes were orange, with dark horizontal slits. Its small ears pricked up like a small dog's when he spoke to it. Its nose was a mere vertical slit at the end of a short muzzle. Its mouth seemed as expressive as a human's; and although it was all but motionless right now, Leonardo sensed that it could smile or purse its lips or do any number of things that no animal he had ever seen could do.

All this the artist saw and mentally registered in the first few seconds. Then he stood aside and studied the little animal again. It was a deep, rich blue, and to the best of his knowledge there was no such thing as a blue animal this side of the bird kingdom.

"Don't move," he said, trying to keep the excitement from his voice. "Just stand there."

He reached out to the door, and very gently, making no sudden movements, he closed it behind the animal. Then, still moving carefully so as not to startle or frighten it, he walked to a nearby bookcase and began pulling out his volumes on animals and nature. One by one he thumbed through them, searching for some indication of exactly what was standing in the corner of his room, watching him curiously.

"What *are* you?" Leonardo repeated as the last of his reference books gave him no hint. Forgotten were Cecilia's portrait, and his flying man, and his war machines. All of his attention was captured by the little blue animal.

"Are you hungry?" he asked at last, as if the animal could answer him.

The creature stared at him, seemingly unafraid, neither approaching him nor backing away.

"Let me see what I have for you," said Leonardo, walking to the kitchen and bringing back a selection of food. "If you would open your mouth, I could tell whether or not you have canines and hence whether you are a carnivore or a herbivore."

The animal's mouth remained closed.

"Well," said Leonardo, "I suppose you are the best judge of what you eat." He lowered himself gently to the floor, moving slowly so as not to startle the animal. "Come, animal," he said gently. "Come and eat."

The creature stared at him curiously but made no attempt to approach him.

"I won't harm you, animal," said Leonardo. "Here, see if this appeals to you." He held out a piece of fish.

The creature took a tentative step toward him, then another. Leonardo remained motionless, studying its movement, trying to figure out how it walked so gracefully with all of its joints in the wrong places. Finally it leaned forward, sniffed at the fish, wrinkled a nose that Leonardo would have sworn couldn't move, and slapped the fish away with a sudden swipe of its forepaw.

"All right, you're not a carnivore—at least, not tonight. Try some fruit."

Leonardo held out a pear. The creature smelled it and then took a small, tentative bite. Evidently it liked what it tasted, because it then took a second, larger bite.

The artist placed the pear on the floor, set another one down next to it, and slowly, carefully got to his feet. While the animal was preoccupied with eating the fruit, Leonardo lit a number of candles and placed them around the room, then went back to his bookcase and tried once more to determine exactly what he was playing host to. After another half hour had passed, he still had no idea.

He picked up a sketchbook and began drawing the little animal, carefully adding notations about the locations of the joints, the lack of canines, the movement of the ears when alerted.

Finally the animal, a slow and delicate eater, had its fill. Leonardo tried to remember if he had closed all his windows, but he needn't have worried. The little creature walked up to him, rubbed against his leg as a cat might, then lay down contentedly atop his shoe.

Leonardo had never had a pet, and he wasn't quite sure what to do; but every instinct told him to lean down and run his hand over the animal's blue fur, and after a moment's hesitation he did just that.

The animal wriggled with pleasure, then rolled onto its back so that he could rub its stomach.

"Well, little friend," said the artist, "if you are to stay for any length of time, I suppose you will need a name." He considered a number of possibilities and then announced: "I will probably never have another pet, so I may as well give you the most impressive name that I know. I shall call you Aristotle, after the great Greek philosopher and scientist." He rubbed the animal's ears. "Do you like that name, Aristotle?"

Aristotle rubbed against him again, which he took as an affirmative.

Leonardo spent the next two hours making more sketches of the little animal, stopping only when he remembered that Aristotle had had nothing to drink since showing up. Leonardo placed a small bowl of water on the floor, then went back to his sketchbook.

When the candles were guttering down, he looked out a window, saw the full moon overhead, and realized that he'd been doing nothing but drawing pictures of Aristotle for the entire evening, his dinner totally forgotten.

"You can't be unique," he murmured. "Surely you had parents; at least one of them must look like you. And from your fearlessness, you are not unacquainted with men. Why is there no drawing or description of you anywhere in my books? Where do you come from?" And again, "What *are* you?"

Aristotle stared up at Leonardo as if fascinated by the sound of his voice.

The artist smiled. "Do you wonder what I am, too?" He yawned and stretched. "Let us go to sleep and attack the problem tomorrow. I hope you are still here in the morning."

He needn't have worried. As he walked to his bedroom, Aristotle fell into step behind him. Leonardo got out of his clothes and spent a few minutes cleaning the ink from his fingers, as he did every night. When he finally walked over to the bed, he found Aristotle sprawled at the foot of it, waiting for him.

"You are obviously someone's loved pet," said Leonardo, climbing into the bed. "He will probably come looking for you in the morning, and I will have to turn you over to him. Still," he added, reaching down and petting the little animal, "I have enjoyed this evening. You do not speak incessantly like Cecilia, nor move endlessly like Prospero. I think, Aristotle, that I would much rather paint you than either of them. What a shame that you will probably be gone tomorrow."

Leonardo was a master of the paintbrush, the sketchbook, and the scientific method . . . but he was a lousy prognosticator.

Machiavelli

Aristotle did not leave the next morning, or the next afternoon, or the day after that. The little creature seemed quite content to remain in Leonardo's home, and gradually the artist found which fruits he would eat and which he wouldn't touch.

Whenever Leonardo sat in front of Cecilia's portrait, Aristotle would hop up onto his lap, content to remain there for as long as Leonardo remained seated. Whenever the artist opened one of his notebooks, Aristotle took it as an invitation to sprawl across the pages.

It was a week after Aristotle had arrived that Leonardo mentioned the odd-looking animal to an acquaintance of his, a minor government employee named Niccolò Machiavelli. When Machiavelli expressed some interest in seeing Aristotle for himself, Leonardo invited him to visit; and the next morning the little civil servant, a small man with dark, piercing eyes, thick lips that always seemed about to sneer, and short, close-cropped hair showed up at the artist's door.

"All right," said Machiavelli. "Where is this remarkable animal whose species you have not yet been able to identify?"

"He'll be in my studio," said Leonardo, leading him there.

Aristotle was sound asleep atop one of the bookshelves. As the two men entered, he opened his eyes and stared curiously at them.

"Stand up so that he can see your legs," said Leonardo.

Aristotle remained motionless, and finally Leonardo walked over and slid a hand under his belly, pressing upward gently until the little animal stood up.

"I've never seen legs like that," remarked Machiavelli.

Aristotle jumped lightly to the floor, walked over to a small bowl of water Leonardo had left out for him, and began drinking.

"Notice how he uses suction, like a horse, rather than lapping it, like a dog or cat," said Leonardo.

Having drunk his fill, Aristotle leaped lightly onto a table where Leonardo had stacked his most recent notebooks, rolled over twice as if scratching his back, and then sat up and watched the two men.

"So what do you think of him, Niccolò?" asked Leonardo.

"I have never seen anything like him," admitted Niccolò Machiavelli.

"Nor have I," agreed Leonardo. "I have made several sketches. Eventually I think I will paint him so that I can properly capture his unique color."

Machiavelli approached Aristotle, studying him intently. Finally he turned back to Leonardo.

"Why not sell him?"

"He's a pet," said Leonardo, surprised.

"The world is filled with things to paint," continued Machiavelli, "but there seems to be only one of this animal. Think of the price he could bring!"

"That's out of the question," replied Leonardo harshly.

"Is it?" said Machiavelli. "Were you not telling me just last week that *il Moro* is months in arrears to you and falling further behind with each passing day? You want to keep your house, and continue using those wildly expensive new kinds of paint, and putter around with your inventions? How long do you think you can continue to do so without money? Here is a perfect opportunity to become wealthy through a single act."

"It's not mine," said Leonardo.

"Oh?" replied Machiavelli. "Whose is it?"

"I don't know."

"Has anyone posted a reward for a missing whatever-he-is?"

"No."

"Have you heard of anyone looking for a lost pet that is neither dog nor cat?"

"You know I haven't."

"Then, since the animal is here, in your house, and no one is searching for it, it is clearly yours to do with as you please." He paused. "For a small commission, I will even handle the sale for you."

"He's not for sale." Leonardo thought of all the money he was owed and of all the money he himself owed. "Not yet, anyway. Not until I'm more desperate than I am now."

"You are making a mistake, my friend," said Machiavelli. "Opportunities to change your life and your fortune are few and far between; and when they present themselves, you must strike before they vanish."

"You sound like a businessman," said the artist.

"A politician," Machiavelli corrected him. Suddenly he smiled. "You are not the only one who keeps notebooks, Leonardo of Vinci. I too write down my thoughts every evening."

"Somehow I suspect that they take very little notice of Art," said Leonardo, returning his smile.

"Absolutely none," agreed Machiavelli.

"Or science."

"Now there you are mistaken, my friend. I believe human behavior, and hence politics, can be dissected and analyzed just like a science."

"Quite possibly it can," said Leonardo noncommittally.

"I do not understand you," said Machiavelli. "You design machines that will kill thousands of the enemy and yet you seem to have no interest in determining who shall wield those machines."

"I have no desire to kill anyone," said Leonardo.

"Yet you design them."

"I am paid more for them than for my art."

"But you are not paid at all," Machiavelli reminded him.

"When I am desperate, *il Moro* releases some money. If I stop working on the machine, the money will stop."

"All the more reason why you should put that brain of yours to work figuring out how to become the next duke."

"Be realistic, Niccolò," said Leonardo. "I am illegitimate. I cannot enter the medical or legal professions. I was not allowed to learn Greek or Latin. Sforza will certainly become the next duke of Milan, and they will remember him long after everyone has forgotten a man named Leonardo."

"At least give some thought to selling the little animal," said Machiavelli.

"I have a feeling you would sell your firstborn," said Leonardo.

"Name a price, and I will answer you," said Machiavelli.

"Be grateful that no one has ever commissioned me to paint a picture of Judas Iscariot," said Leonardo with a smile. "He might look uncomfortably like you.""No he won't," said Machiavelli. "Judas chose the wrong side. I would never do that."

"No," agreed Leonardo. "I suppose you wouldn't."

Machiavelli reached out and laid a hand on the artist's shoulder. "Let me know if you change your mind."

He turned and left the house, and Leonardo returned to Cecilia's portrait, dabbing here, touching up there, still dissatisfied not with the painting but with the concept of the painting, the time it was taking him, time that could have been better spent on more challenging projects.

A moment later Aristotle hopped onto his lap, and Leonardo absently ran his fingers through the animal's blue fur while he studied the unfinished painting.

Before long he arose, walked over to his notebooks, and began thumbing through them. There was a notion he'd had a week or two ago, one that had inspired a preliminary drawing he'd been thinking about on and off ever since: a device that would allow a man to float gently to the ground from an enormous height.

True, he was still stymied about how to get his man to that height; but once he was up there, he'd need a safe means of descent, and Leonardo knew that his subconscious mind would be working on the flight problem while his conscious was working on this one. He studied his drawing, then made a few changes and added some notes.

Satisfied, he went to his bookshelves and tried, for perhaps the hundredth time, to identify Aristotle's species or if not that, at least his general family. After an hour he gave up, still unable to made any headway at all.

Then a thought occurred to him. Possibly no animal of Aristotle's species had ever been domesticated before. That didn't mean there wouldn't be descriptions of it. He put his scientific texts back on the shelf and pulled out three memoirs of travelers and explorers. Perhaps the answer would be there.

He sat down on a chair and began reading. Soon the words began to blur, and he decided to rest his eyes for just a moment. He closed them and leaned back, the book laid across his lap.

When he opened his eyes again it was daylight, and he realized he'd been asleep for almost ten hours. He got up, stretched, put the books back, and looked around for Aristotle. The animal was nowhere to be found.

Concerned, Leonardo began walking through the entire house, searching each room. No Aristotle.

A frightening thought cross his mind. *If Niccolò has stolen him to sell . . .*

They were friends, but he wouldn't put it past Machiavelli. He wouldn't put anything past Machiavelli.

He would look once more and then confront Niccolò and demand his pet back.

Another quick search of the house proved fruitless. He opened the front door to see if perhaps the little animal had somehow crawled out through a window, but there was nothing there.

He decided to make one last attempt. "Here, Aristotle," he called again. "Here, boy."

He was seconds from leaving for Machiavelli's house when he heard a heavily accented voice say: "You're never going to get a response if you keep using the wrong name *and* the wrong sex."

Melody

Leonardo turned and found himself facing a boy in his teens dressed in the fashion of the day. His hair, his accent, everything seemed somehow *wrong*, yet the boy didn't seem threatening. The artist studied him, trying to pinpoint the anomalies.

"Her name is Melody," said the boy.

"The animal is a male, and his name is Aristotle," said Leonardo.

The boy smiled in amusement. "Her name is Melody," he repeated, "and she is well named. Are you having trouble finding her?"

Leonardo merely stared at him without answering.

"Watch—and listen," said the boy.

He pursed his lips and whistled a simple tune—and suddenly there was a melodic response, not human but infinitely more beautiful. The boy walked toward the source of the music and soon found the little animal where it had been asleep beneath a pile of clothing in Leonardo's bedroom.

"You see?" said the boy, picking up the animal in his arms and carrying it back to the studio. "This is Melody. She ran away from me last week. Thank you for caring for her."

"Who are you and where are you from?" demanded the artist. "And what kind of animal is Melody?"

"I'm not allowed to tell you," said the boy, heading toward the front door with Melody in his arms—but Leonardo got there first and barred his way.

"I want answers," he said.

"I've got to leave."

"Not before we talk," said Leonardo. "Let's begin with you. You're no native to Milan, but I can't identify your accent. Where are you from?"

"Florence."

"Nonsense. The citizens of Florence have no accent."

"I can't help that," said the boy. "Florence is where I come from."

"Dressed like this?"

"Yes."

"I have never seen you before," said Leonardo. "I have done you no harm. Why do you come into my house spouting all these obvious lies?"

"I haven't lied to you, Leonardo."

"And how do you know my name?"

"I know all about you," said the boy. "I know you were born on April 15, 1452. I know your mother's name is Caterina. I know that you were charged with a crime against Nature in Florence on April 9, 1476, and that the case was dismissed on June 16 of the same year. I know—"

"Enough!" snapped Leonardo. He studied the boy carefully. "All right—so you've been to Florence long enough to study the court records. That doesn't mean you live there, and from your appearance you clearly do not. Who are you, and how do you know so many details of my life?"

"You wouldn't believe me if I told you."

"I am an intelligent man. Try me."

The boy sighed. "I can't."

"Then we'll stay here together until you can," replied Leonardo.

"I've got to get back."

"After you answer my questions."

"I can't," said the boy. "It isn't permitted."

"Permitted?" repeated Leonardo. "Permitted by whom?"

"It wouldn't make any sense to you even if I told you," said the boy.

"I have all day," said Leonardo. "I'm not going anywhere. Are you?"

"All right," said the boy with another sigh. "I am not permitted to answer you by order of the Trans-Temporal Authority."

"That is meaningless."

"I told you it wouldn't make any sense to you."

"Then explain it so I can understand it," said Leonardo.

The boy shook his head firmly. "It could cause serious problems if I did."

"You come to my house, you know things about my past that no one in Milan knows, you know things about my pet that even *I* don't know. . . . I can't let you leave without some answers."

"She's *my* pet!" the boy shot back heatedly.

His voice startled Melody, who jumped to the floor and scurried over to Leonardo.

"Perhaps we'll let *him* decide who he belongs to," said Leonardo. "And while we're on the subject, why do you persist in calling him a female?"

"I can't tell you."

"I won't let you leave until you do," said Leonardo, lowering himself to the floor and sitting cross-legged with his back against the door, his right hand idly stroking Melody's blue fur. "Let me know when you're hungry."

The boy sat down, also cross-legged, about fifteen feet from Leonardo.

They were silent for almost ten minutes. The boy made no motion to leave, and Leonardo made no motion to threaten him.

"Antares," said the boy at last.

"Antares?"

"It's a star. When night falls, perhaps someone can point it out to you."

"All right, it's a star," said Leonardo, wondering where this was leading.

"That's where Melody's from—the fourth planet circling Antares. I don't know the scientific name for her species. We just call them Singers. Some of them eat vegetables, but she prefers fruit."

"You have quite an imagination," said Leonardo.

"Okay," said the boy irritably. "Where do *you* think she's from?"

"I don't know."

"Have you ever seen another animal like her?" persisted the boy.

"Have you ever seen one with blue fur, or heard one who could sing like Melody can? Have you ever seen one with legs like hers?"

"No, I have not," admitted Leonardo. He stared thoughtfully at the little animal. "Perhaps someone has beaten Columbus to India and returned with him."

"There are animals in the Americas that no one has ever seen before, but she is not one of them."

"The Americas?" repeated Leonardo. "What are the Americas?"

"The land masses of the New World."

"Hah!" cried Leonardo so suddenly that Melody jumped in surprise. "The New World is *not* India, is it? I *knew* it!"

"No, it is not India," confirmed the boy. "But they will not know it, and they will call the race of people they find there Indians."

"You speak with such authority," noted Leonardo, "yet Columbus has not yet departed. I think you are a great teller of tales."

"No," said the boy. "What I am is a very average student of history."

"History is what happened in the past," said Leonardo. "Columbus's voyage is still in the future."

"*Your* future," said the boy. "*My* past."

Leonardo stared at him for a long moment. "You are either a lunatic or you are telling the truth. If the former, I must summon the police and have them return you to wherever it is you escaped from. But you seem friendly enough and have not threatened me with any physical harm, so in the interest of science, I will, for the moment, assume you are telling the truth."

"I can prove it to you," said the boy. He got up, walked over to

Leonardo and gently took Melody from the artist, and then laid the little animal on its back. "What you took for a male organ is actually an extendable protective device to shield her children from the extremely rocky surface of her home planet when they cling to her belly, upside down, in their infancy." He demonstrated. "Do you see?"

"Amazing!" muttered Leonardo.

The boy held out an arm. "Do you want more proof? Examine the cloth of my sleeve."

Leonardo felt the cloth, pulled it gently, studied its texture.

The boy's gaze fell upon Melody's water dish. He walked over, picked it up, and brought it back. When he was a step away from the artist, he poured it on his forearm, then knelt down.

"Examine it again," said the boy, extending his arm.

"It's dry!" exclaimed Leonardo.

"Have you ever seen a zipper before?"

"A zipper?" repeated Leonardo.

"Watch."

The boy unzipped his coat, then zipped it again.

"Remarkable!" said the artist.

"Just like magic," said the boy.

"I don't believe in magic," replied Leonardo. "It is obviously science—but a science with which I am unacquainted."

Melody jumped onto Leonardo's lap and rubbed against him. "So men will reach the stars!" he whispered, staring at the little animal.

"Almost a century before I was born."

"Tell me more!" said Leonardo eagerly, like a man thirsting for water in the desert. "Tell me of all the wonders the future holds! Do men still fight wars? Have we conquered disease? Does the church still dominate the minds of men?"

"I've already told you more than I should," said the boy uneasily.

"You can't stop!" said Leonardo desperately. "Now that you have convinced me that you are what you claim to be, you can't leave without answering all my questions!"

"I'm in big trouble already," said the boy. "If anyone finds out that I've come here looking for Melody . . ." He shuddered inadvertently. "I've got to go back."

I can't lose this opportunity! thought the artist. *Think, Leonardo! Think!*

And suddenly his course of action became clear to him.

"All right," said Leonardo, getting to his feet while still holding Melody. "I won't stop you."

"Thank you," said the boy. "I'm sorry to have troubled you, and I thank you for watching my pet for me." He reached out his hands. "May I have her back now?"

"*You* are free to go," said the artist, feeling guilty and excited at the same time, because he knew his plan would work. "Melody stays here."

"I can't go back without her," said the boy desperately. "She's the reason I'm here!"

"Then I think we'd better come to an agreement," said Leonardo.

FIVE

Mario

The boy looked around the room, panic-stricken.

"Relax," said Leonardo. "I'm not going to harm you or Melody, and you're not going to get into any trouble."

"I'm *already* in trouble!" shouted the boy. "You don't understand!"

"Then explain," said Leonardo. "I'm a fast learner."

"I can't tell you!"

"I already know that you come from the future," said Leonardo.

The boy stared at him as if trying to make up his mind.

Finally he sighed, and all the tension seemed to flow out of his lean body. "All right," he said. "My name is Mario Ravelli, and I really do live in Florence." He paused, staring at the artist, as if hoping that something, anything, would stop him from uttering his next sentence. "But I live there in the year of Our Lord 2523."

"It's comforting to know that Florence still stands and men still live there a thousand years from now," said Leonardo.

"Anyway," continued Mario unhappily, "they perfected time

travel in 2481 A.D. We're not allowed to interact with anyone or anything in the past, because that might change the future. For example, if I see a rock in the road and move it onto the grass at the roadside so no wheels will be broken on it, perhaps a horse will injure a foot on it in the dark and his rider will be thrown, and because of the fall the man will not meet the woman he would otherwise have encountered at a ball that evening, and hence he will not marry her and a great doctor or writer may never be born. Do you see?"

"Yes, it's obvious," said Leonardo. "But why is a young boy allowed to travel through time by himself? Why is there no supervision?"

"There is," said Mario. "Usually." He paused uneasily. "But nobody knows I'm here."

The artist smiled. "I thought not."

"This trip was my present for graduating at the head of my class," said Mario, not without a note of pride. "It took a lot of my family's savings to come back in time and visit the Renaissance."

"What is the Renaissance?"

"It is the period in which you live, or at least that's the name we know it by," explained Mario. "I thought I'd like it better than I do. I don't know how you put up with it. Most of the people still live in squalor, disease runs rampant, nations still go to war."

"Then what is it that makes the Renaissance so important that people from a thousand years in the future wish to visit it?"

"Europe has been asleep for centuries," answered Mario. "It is here and now that it finally begins to wake up."

"And I have something to do with that?" asked Leonardo.

The boy stared at him but refused to answer.

"Come, come, Mario," said the artist. "You know my name, you know my history, you probably even know the name of the model I am currently painting. Obviously I am one of the men you came here to observe."

The boy nodded his head unhappily.

"But you are without your family or any other travelers," said Leonardo. "What is the reason?"

"Melody is my pet," replied Mario.

"So you told me."

"She ran off during the last day of our visit," said Mario miserably. "I only noticed that she was missing after we arrived back in my era. That's when I knew I had to come back and get her. I can't let people see her, and start wondering where she came from." His face became almost pleading. "I have to take her home with me."

"I know."

"And I have to do it fast, before anyone notices I've gone," continued Mario, trying to keep the panic from his voice. "I've already broken the law by sneaking into the trans-temporal transporter on my own. If I don't get back fast, I could go to jail. Maybe my whole family could."

"No one is going to jail, Mario," said Leonardo. "If I can prove that to you, will you listen to my proposition?"

"How can you prove it?" demanded the boy. "You don't know how strict the Trans-Temporal Authority can be."

"It makes no difference," said the artist placidly. "If I show you that there is a way in which no harm will befall you or your family, will you listen?"

The boy checked his timepiece, which seemed to be bonded to his wrist. "I've already been here four hours," he said. "Someone will have noticed."

Leonardo pointed to the timepiece. "That device tells you the hour?"

"And the minute, and the second."

"Amazing."

"And it tells me that they've already had time to notice my absence."

"You are not looking at this like a scientist," said Leonardo gently.

"I'm *not* a scientist!" snapped Mario. "I'm a boy who has messed up his whole life and is probably going to jail!"

"Let us see how bright a boy you are," said Leonardo. "How did you know that you would find Melody at this particular place, on this particular day?"

"It is the fourteenth day of May," said Mario. "We left Milan and returned home on the morning of May 14, 1490 A.D."

"And knowing that, you were able to somehow transport yourself back to the very hour you left?"

"Yes."

Leonardo smiled. "Well, there you have it."

"Have what?"

"The solution to your problem."

"I don't know what you're talking about!"

"*Think*, boy!" urged Leonardo. "You graduated at the top of your class, so you clearly have a brain. Now, you were able to choose the very second you arrived, were you not?"

"Yes, I just told you that."

"And even if you had been at home for a week or a month or a year, you could have chosen the very same instant to visit Milan again?"

"Yes."

"Well, then?" asked Leonardo.

Suddenly Mario returned his smile. "I never thought of that!" he exclaimed excitedly. "Just because I've been here for four hours doesn't mean I have to return home four hours after I left! I can go back one second after I left, and no one will even know I was gone!"

"You see?" said Leonardo. "All problems are capable of solution."

"Thank you for pointing it out! You're as brilliant as they say!"

"Do they say that?" asked Leonardo, looking inordinately pleased.

"You are the greatest thinker, and one of the two greatest artists, of the Renaissance."

"Oh? And who is the other?"

"You don't know him," said Mario. "At least, not yet."

"I know the work of every fine artist in Italy."

"Not this one," replied Mario. "He's only fifteen years old."

"What is his name?"

"I can't tell you."

"I promise that I will make no attempt to influence him or his work," said Leonardo. "I just want to know when he begins to produce it."

"You'll know it," said Mario with conviction. "The whole world will know it."

"He's that good?"

"He will be."

"Then if I will recognize his talent instantly, why can you not reveal his name?"

"I don't know. I just know that I can't."

We will try again later, after you learn to trust me more, thought Leonardo. *But I must know who this other great artist is. Maybe I can help him—or, better still, learn from him.*

"Well, young Mario," said Leonardo aloud, "are you ready to hear my proposition?"

"You've kept Melody safe for me and probably kept me out of jail as well," answered Mario. "I owe it to you at least to listen."

"You are interested in this place and time. I, Leonardo da Vinci, will introduce you as my distant cousin, and will give you a tour such as you could never receive from someone of your era. They might know which people have historical significance, but they cannot introduce you to the people. Come with me and I will take you through the streets of Milan, let you watch and listen as I visit with my friends. I will invite you to observe me as I work and ask any questions you wish, and I will answer them as fully as I can. You can stay until my patron and my model return from Naples in three weeks. My servant and apprentices will be gone for most of that time, so we will not have to explain your presence to them. When you are ready to leave, I will not stop you, nor prevent you from taking Melody with you."

Three weeks in this place? thought Mario. *Three weeks without a chemical shower? Without soya products flavored and colored to my taste? Freezing when it's cold, burning when it's hot, getting soaked when it rains? Wearing the same clothes, drinking unfiltered water?*

What if I get sick? Do they still bleed patients with leeches?

All that's on the one hand. On the other is a chance to live in Leonardo's house every day, to watch him work, to see if there's really anything to the Renaissance besides disease, poverty, and a handful of gifted artists.

"Nothing's ever that simple," said Mario at last. "What must I do for my part of the deal?"

Leonardo got to his feet and walked over to a stack of his notebooks. He picked up one, opened it, and quickly flipped through the pages.

"I have hundreds, perhaps thousands, of drawings, of ideas and inventions, in these booklets. The problem is that I do not have the money to bring most of them into being, or even to build prototypes to determine whether they actually work as designed. You will examine the drawings, and where the concepts are flawed you will tell me how to correct them. Have we a bargain?"

Mario shook his head. "I already told you: I can't give you any knowledge that might change the future."

"What if I promised not to act on any information you gave me?" asked Leonardo.

"Tell me the truth," said Mario. "Could you keep that promise?"

Leonardo was silent for a moment. "No," he admitted at last. "No, I could not."

"I didn't think so."

"I cannot keep you here against your will," said Leonardo. "And of course you can take Melody with you. I am sorry to have caused you such distress. It was my eagerness to know if my machines will work."

"It seems a shame to leave now that I know that I can return just seconds after I departed," said the boy. "To be so close to actually seeing you at work . . ." Suddenly his face brightened. "Are you open to a counter-offer?"

"Let me hear it."

"I won't tell you *how* to make your machines work," said Mario. "That would alter the future, and we both know why I can't do that. But what I *can* do is look at your drawings and tell you which ones will work and which ones won't. If I don't tell you *why* they won't, that won't be altering anything, will it?"

"A smart boy *and* a moral boy. I think we are going to become good friends." Leonardo extended his hand. "Mario Ravelli, I accept your terms."

CHAPTER

Portrait

"One of the unhappy truths an artist or a scientist must acknowledge is that you cannot always do what you want or work on the project that most interests you," remarked Leonardo, as he led Mario into his studio. "For example, I would love to spend the next few years perfecting my flying machines, but my patron is the Regent of Milan, and if I am to remain here, I must provide him with his war machines." He paused. "This is not to say that the creation of these machines isn't challenging, but rather that I am distressed by the uses to which they will be put."

"Then say no," said Mario.

Leonardo shook his head sadly. "I do not know what things will be like a thousand years from now; but should I defy a direct order of Ludovico Sforza, I will not even know what things will be like tomorrow, for he will certainly have me killed tonight. I am a thinker and a painter, not a warrior. I cannot withstand an army all by myself, nor would I wish to live in hiding, away from my paints and my notebooks and my books. So," he concluded with a shrug, "when he says he wants war machines, I create war machines—at least on paper." He stopped before the painting of Cecilia. "And when he says he wants his mistress painted, I paint his mistress."

"I see," said Mario noncommittally.

"*Lady with a Cat*," said Leonardo. "That is what I have tentatively called it." Suddenly the artist turned to the boy. "Did it survive the century?"

"You know I can't tell you that."

Leonardo sighed. "I know. I wasn't even thinking of the painting itself but of the process."

"The process?" asked Mario.

"I have mixed my paints with oils," explained the artist. "A few others have used oils in the past, but I have created new mixtures, new textures, new methods of preserving the paints. The colors are both richer and more subtle; and based on my calculations, every painting I create should outlive me if it isn't destroyed. That was my real question: Will the *process* survive?"

"That much I think I can tell you," said Mario.

"Well?" said Leonardo eagerly.

"They still use oils a thousand years from now. Not everyone, but some of them. A few, anyway."

"I knew it!" cried Leonardo happily. "Thank you, Mario, my young friend! They laughed at me when I was an apprentice, and they ridiculed the notion of paints mixed with oil. I cannot tell you how gratifying it is to know that my method will triumph!" He couldn't hold still, and began walking excitedly around the studio. "So they will still paint with oils all those many years from now! Isn't that remarkable!" He picked Melody up. "And if you hadn't wandered into my house, I would never know that! How can I thank you?"

"Try feeding her some grapes," suggested Mario. "Or maybe a plum."

"She shall have all that and more," said Leonardo. "But she would have that anyway. I must find some special way to thank her. Something unique. Something . . ."

He seemed lost in thought for a moment. Melody became restless and wriggled free, jumping lightly to the floor. Leonardo didn't seem to even notice she had left his arms.

"Are you all right?" asked Mario after another minute had passed.

"Something unique," Leonardo repeated, half whispering. "Something that will help me remember of Melody after you have taken her away." Suddenly his eyes fell on Cecilia's unfinished portrait. "I have it!" he shouted so forcefully that Mario literally jumped.

"What is it?" asked the boy.

"Do you remember what I just told you about doing my patron's bidding?"

"Yes."

"Well, he commissioned a painting of Cecilia Gallerani, which is exactly the same as ordering me to paint it upon pain of death or banishment if I refused; but he did *not* order me to paint Prospero."

"Prospero?"

"That horrible cat," said Leonardo, unable to keep his dislike for the cat out of his voice. "I think today I will remove him from the painting and substitute Melody instead. I have enough sketches of her that I will not need her to pose with Cecilia. She is almost the same size as Prospero; it should not prove too difficult a task, and I have almost three weeks to do it before Sforza and Cecilia return from Naples."

"Can you complete it by then?" asked Mario.

"I'll paint with both hands if I have to," replied the artist.

"That was a serious question," said Mario.

"And I gave you a serious answer," said Leonardo. "I have taught myself to write and paint with either hand, though to be honest I favor my left hand." He paused. "I can write with my left hand while painting with my right."

"Really?" Mario looked around the walls of the studio, which were covered with sketches and notes. "Which of these did you do that way?"

"None."

"None?"

"I threw them all away." Leonardo smiled. "The fact that I can write and paint at the same time does not mean, alas, that my writing is legible or my painting acceptable. But I am working on improving my skills."

"I'm impressed that you can do it at all," said Mario.

"I can do many useless tricks," said Leonardo, who seemed anything but impressed with himself. "I can even write in both directions."

"I know that. But I don't know why."

"I hold the pen with my left hand," explained Leonardo, "and when I write across the paper the normal way, the heel of my hand smudges the ink. But I found that if I write from right to left, this doesn't happen." Suddenly he grinned. "It also keeps my notes and inventions secret."

"We call that mirror writing," said Mario. "You have to hold a mirror up to it to be able to read it. Mostly it's done by geniuses and madmen."

"You will forgive me if I don't ask you which one I am," said Leonardo with a smile.

"History wouldn't know of you if you were a madman."

"Thank you for that, and I shall go out of my way not to mention Caligula." He turned to Cecilia's portrait again. "I shall have to consider this very carefully. Although they are the same size and weight, Melody is not shaped exactly like Prospero. I must figure out her exact position before I insert her into the painting."

"I could hold her, and you could pretend I was Cecilia," suggested Mario.

"You arms are longer, your fingers broader, your clothing sits differently upon you," replied Leonardo. "I compose my paintings with the geometric proportions and mathematical principles that were originally discovered by the Greeks during the time of Plato and Aristotle."

"What principles?" asked Mario curiously, staring at the painting.

"This one utilizes the concept of the pyramid," explained the artist. "This is how I am creating the portrait, broadest at the bottom of the painting, with all proportions narrowing to the top of her head."

"I see," said Mario.

"Now tell me what you *don't* see," said Leonardo.

Mario frowned. "I don't understand."

"What don't you see in the painting?"

"I don't know," said the boy with a shrug. "I don't see an elephant."

"Be serious."

"I don't know what you want me to say."

"Look at it carefully," said Leonardo. "What you will not see is a natural straight line. Every line in the painting is curved, except for the artificial lines of Cecilia's neckline and headband."

"I never noticed that!" said Mario.

Leonardo smiled. "You weren't supposed to. But your eyes are windows to your soul, and that is where it is supposed to register."

"You mean my subconscious."

"Is that what they call it? I suppose it is as good a word as any. Anyway, tell me what else you see."

"Just the woman and the cat."

"True," agreed the artist. "But *how* do you see them?"

"With my eyes," said Mario. "But you can't mean that. I'm confused again. What do you want me to say?"

"Anyone can paint a woman and a cat," said Leonardo patiently. "But it takes a certain subtle skill to make you see them the way I *want* you to see them. Observe those curved lines we spoke about. They carry the viewer's gaze from Cecilia's head down her left arm, across the cat, and back up her right arm to her face again. You don't realize it consciously, but that is the way you look at the painting, because that is the way my choice of geometric patterns and curved lines has forced you to look at it."

"I never knew that," admitted Mario, staring at the painting and realizing that was precisely the way he looked at it.

"And that is why I must be so careful inserting Melody into the painting in place of Prospero," continued Leonardo. "If a single curve is wrong, the eye will stop on her and not continue its journey back to Cecilia's face."

"I never realized painting was so scientific," said Mario. "I just assumed artists were born with the gift of painting or sculpting and that was that. I didn't know how much planning went into it."

"Do they play music in your era?" asked Leonardo.

"Yes, of course they do."

"And the man or woman with the most beautiful voice—is that voice totally untrained? Did its possessor not study with masters and rehearse constantly?"

"Yes, of course," said Mario. "I just never thought much about it before."

"There are painters who can create a portrait in a day," said Leonardo. "I have taken more than a year on this one. I would like to think that even the casual observer can see that there is a difference in quality."

"I hope you'll keep telling me what you're doing and why," said Mario. "The little bit you've told me today is fascinating, and I'd like to learn more."

"That is part of our bargain," agreed Leonardo. "Perhaps I will even let you help me mix my paints."

"I'd enjoy that."

"And if you see any inefficiencies in the process, perhaps you can—"

"You know I can't," interrupted the boy.

"I don't ask you to make me a better painter," said Leonardo. "Just one whose paintings might last beyond his lifetime."

"They will. I've already told you that much."

"All of them?"

"I'm sure all of them will outlive you," answered Mario carefully. "That's a far cry from surviving all the way to my era."

"But some will?"

Mario stared at him silently.

"I'm sorry," said Leonardo. "I should not have asked." He walked briskly across the studio. "Come, young Mario. It is time I started keeping my end of the agreement. Come and see a world that is finally awakening from its long, dark slumber."

Mario followed him, and a moment later the painter and the boy were walking down the streets of Milan.

SEVEN

Milan

"Is it not a beautiful city?" said Leonardo.

"It's impressive," answered Mario noncommittally, trying to get used to all the strange odors attacking his nostrils. Many were repugnant, a few were intriguing, but all were unnerving to a boy who'd grown up with only artificial and manufactured scents.

Mario stepped around a muddy puddle. *I wonder: Do they even have sewers, or is that what I'm afraid it is?*

"I would live nowhere else," continued Leonardo. "Are any of the structures still standing in your era?"

"A couple."

Leonardo smiled. "But you cannot tell me which."

"No, I can't."

"Have you built anything as magnificent as these?"

You see magnificence, thought Mario. *I see stairs instead of anti-grav lifts, I see vermin hiding in dark corners, I see dirt everywhere. Not a single building is self-cleaning. I dont know how anyone lives to adulthood in these conditions, or even why they'd want to.*

Aloud the boy said, "A couple."

"Then let me take you to the ones I think are most likely to sur-vive," said the artist. "And whether I am right or wrong, you will see the best that Milan has to offer in this 1490th year of Our Lord. Almost every street is paved, and we even hire men to clean all the horse manure off the pavement once a day."

"I'm impressed," said Mario. *Well, compared to most of the cities in the world, I guess it is impressive.*

"We will begin with the castle of my patron," said Leonardo, heading off to his left. They passed a number of food stalls, and the artist stopped at a fruit vendor. He bought each of them a pear, and then they continued walking. Mario had no intention of eating a piece of fruit that anyone might have touched, and tossed it away when Leonardo wasn't looking.

Most of the people they saw seemed to know Leonardo, and he had a word of greeting for each of them. Mario was surprised at the number of dogs and cats running loose. They passed a trio of artists displaying their work, and Leonardo had a word of encouragement for each of them.

The area thinned out somewhat, and finally the artist turned to the boy. "Are you a hunter, Mario?"

"No," said Mario as an expression of distaste crossed his face.

"I am told it is a wonderful sport for a young man."

"You are told?" repeated the boy. "That sounds like you have not experienced it yourself."

"No, I was too busy with other things."

"Well, I am not too busy," replied Mario. "But the world has changed between your time and mine. Hunting became so popular that there are almost no wild animals left, and those that remain are strictly protected. The penalties for killing one of them are so great that no one would dream of hunting."

Leonardo looked surprised. "What kind of weapons must you have in the twenty-sixth century?"

"We killed four-fifths of them before the start of the twenty-first century," answered the boy. "They say that in the twentieth century alone, we killed more than sixteen million elephants in Africa and another two million in Asia."

"I hope my machines were not responsible for this carnage!" said Leonardo fervently.

"No, they weren't."

They walked in silence for a few minutes, Leonardo with a troubled expression on his face. Finally he turned to Mario.

"If men could do that to animals, what are they capable of doing to each other?"

"You don't want to know."

"I don't *want* to," agreed the artist. "But I must."

"In the year 1945, we developed a weapon that killed seventy thousand men and women in about ten seconds," said Mario. "And ten years later we had developed so many more deadly weapons that it was obsolete. Today we have the ability to instantly vaporize any planet in the solar system."

"And yet the race survived for another six centuries!" said Leonardo. "Amazing!"

"Thank you."

"For what?"

"For not asking me the nature of the weapon," said Mario.

You know, he thought, *there are worse things than not having the technology to destroy the race.*

Leonardo took a final bite of his pear, then offered the core to a donkey that was left standing alone attached to a two-wheeled cart, while its master was conducting business elsewhere. Mario was about to pet the animal when he saw some flies crawling across its head and promptly pulled back his hand, wondering once again why the whole world hadn't come down with disease.

"The reason I asked you about hunting," said Leonardo, rejoining the boy, "is because of this park that we are approaching." He point ed ahead to a vast expanse of green.

"There must be a thousand birds there," remarked Mario. "I could hear them for the last half mile."

"The remnants of the Visconti Ducal garden, which was created more than a century ago," answered the artist. "It is now a seven-hundred-hectare hunting preserve owned by *il Moro*. I have been invited to hunt in it, though I have always refused. I thought if you were a hunter, you might care to partake of its sport."

"In my era, killing animals isn't sport," said Mario. "It's a crime that ranks just below murder." He peered past some shrubbery. "What kinds of animals live there?"

"*Il Moro* has imported antelope from northern Africa, and for a while he had a pair of lions, but they were killed three years ago."

"Nice fellow, your patron," said Mario.

"You don't reach his position of power by being a nice fellow," answered Leonardo. "And he will surely become the next duke."

They began walking through the park. Mario caught sight of a doe and fawn in the distance, and a variety of colorful birds were stalking through the grass, looking for insects.

"It's lovely here," said the boy, and realized to his surprise that he was telling the truth. It would be lovelier without the dirt and the insects and the humidity; but this was the first time he'd ever been in a truly natural park, unenhanced by artificial sounds and smells, totally unsterilized, and he decided that he could grow used to it without any difficulty. It was a disturbing thought for a boy of his era.

"I often come here to put my thoughts in order," replied Leonardo. He grimaced. "And to see my patron. His castle is just beyond the park."

It took them another ten minutes to cross the park, and then a huge stone structure seemed to rise up out of the ground.

"Sforza's palace?" asked Mario.

"His castle," Leonardo replied. "Castle Sforzesco."

"It's huge." *I wonder if it has indoor plumbing, but I guess it would be rude to ask.*

"It was originally built more than one hundred years ago," said Leonardo. "It was torn down and rebuilt by one of my patron's predecessors, Francesco Sforza, when I was a small child. Do you see how nothing grows within hundreds of meters of it? That is so nothing can obstruct the army's vision if the castle is attacked, and at the same time the terrain affords the enemy no cover. The cylindrical towers give *il Moro's* men a further advantage, for his army will be positioned there and atop the walls that encircle the castle. Note the small windows, which is his men's only point of vulnerability. Most of their bodies are hidden behind the stone walls, protected from the enemy's weapons."

"It looks impregnable," said Mario.

"For men of my century, but doubtless not of yours."

"True."

"Come inside the walls, and we will take a closer look," said Leonardo. He signaled to a guard, who opened a small door in the wall and let them through.

"Another tower," noted Mario.

A group of crows were eating something very small and very dead at the far end of the courtyard. He stared at the birds in horrified fascination.

"It is called the Torre di Bona after Bona di Savoia, one of the former residents of the castle."

"That's quite a moat surrounding it," said Mario, glad to have his attention taken away from the feasting birds. "Is there anything dangerous swimming in it?"

"Not to my knowledge," answered Leonardo. "There certainly wasn't anything in it when I built the bridge across it."

Mario stared at the bridge. "*You* built that?"

Leonardo looked amused. "Is it so difficult to believe?"

"No. It's just that I didn't know that. There are so many books about you, so many disks and cubes . . . I must have missed the ones that mentioned it."

"There are many books, you say?" asked Leonardo happily.

"Yes."

"What are disks and cubes?"

Mario smiled. "They are things that aren't books."

"All right. I apologize for asking." Leonardo looked at the castle thoughtfully. "I think we will not enter it," he announced at last. "Sforza would ask too many questions about you when he returns, and I am not a facile liar."

"Where shall we go next?"

"There are two more structures I should like to show you today," said the artist. "Are you getting tired? It is quite some distance."

"I'm ready."

"Good, because whether you are from Naples or Florence or the twenty-sixth century, you really should see these buildings while you are in Milan. I am sure they must have survived into your era."

"Why them and not Sforza's castle?" asked Mario as they began walking.

"Because they are religious edifices. The castle is a military structure, and it is not difficult to believe that it will be captured and destroyed in the next thousand years, or even the next hundred—but who would destroy churches?"

"That's probably what the Egyptians thought too," said Mario.

"I don't understand the reference," said Leonardo, suddenly interested. "Please explain."

"The Egyptians worshipped many gods, and carved and painted representations of them on all their temples. When they were conquered, the Christian soldiers defaced all the statues and paintings they could find so that none of the gods had faces."

"I did not know this."

"I'm pretty hazy on my Middle Eastern history," said Mario

uneasily. "Perhaps it hasn't happened yet."

"I have no intention of ever going to Egypt," said Leonardo reassuringly. "I promise that it shall remain our secret."

"Thank you."

Leonardo looked ahead and saw a man approaching. "This is Ambrogio de Predis, a fellow artist," he said softly. "Be silent and let me do the talking. It would be difficult to explain your accent."

Leonardo waved to Ambrogio, they exchanged greetings, and Leonardo introduced Mario as the mute son of a friend from Venice who would be visiting for a few days, then breathed a sigh of relief when the artist bade him farewell and continued on his way.

They walked in silence for another half hour, Leonardo resisting the urge to ask a hundred questions about the future, Mario fearful that he might thoughtlessly blurt out an answer to such questions. The streets became more crowded, the houses more impressive, and the boy tried to adjust to the sudden onslaught of noise and odors.

Finally they arrived at the Monastery of St. Ambrose, a brick structure that possessed a pair of matching towers that were even higher than the castle's.

"Who was Saint Ambrose?" asked Mario as they came to a halt in front of the building.

"He was a bishop in this area," explained Leonardo. "He lived even further in my past than you do in my future."

"And have you done any work on this building?"

"I can't work on *everything*," said Leonardo. "I wonder what lies your books have told about me."

"I wish I could discuss them with you and find out," replied Mario, "but . . ."

"I know, I know," Leonardo sighed. "Well, let us see the last thing I wish to show you today, and then it will be time for some reciprocity."

"Reciprocity?" repeated Mario, puzzled.

Leonardo nodded. "Yes. I am keeping my end of the bargain. Soon it will be your turn, and I will finally learn if I can make a man fly."

How difficult can it be? thought the artist with renewed confidence. *After all, you have reached the stars. Surely I can make a man soar a mere fifteen meters above the ground.*

EIGHT

Color

Suddenly there was a clap of thunder, and a minute later rain began pouring down. It was the first time Mario had ever been rained on; he decided that he didn't like it.

"I think we'll look at the Cathedral some other day," said Leonardo, ducking into a doorway.

"I'm all turned around," said Mario. "How far do you live from here?"

"Perhaps a five-minute walk," said the artist. Then: "Can they control the weather in the future?"

"Pretty much."

"What a shame, to lose the beauty of a rainbow, or the dusting of snow on the ground on a winter day."

"It is really that pretty?"

Leonardo smiled. "It is magnificent, not only for its beauty but also for its unpredictability."

"Maybe," said Mario, "but at least we can prevent the glaciers from spreading in the next ice age."

"Ice age?" repeated Leonardo.

Mario grimaced. "Forget I said it. You and I will both be dead for thousands of years before it happens—*if* it happens." He looked out at the street. "The rain seems to have let up for the moment. Shall we go?"

"By all means," said Leonardo, beginning to walk at a very fast pace. "I can't tell you how resentful I will be to die without seeing all the wonders of your era."

"They don't seem like wonders to us," answered the boy. "A cave-man, or even an ancient Greek or Roman, would probably find the Renaissance just as wonderful and incomprehensible."

"The incomprehensible interests me not at all," replied Leonardo. "But the things that I *might* comprehend . . . that is a different matter." He paused for a moment, as if considering his next remark. "May I say something that will perhaps sound pompous?"

"Go ahead."

"You mentioned that Europe was waking from a long slumber. Sometimes I feel that I am the only one who has thus far opened his eyes. I would give anything to have someone of equal intellect to exchange ideas with."

"I don't think anyone's ever been your equal," said Mario. "Or ever will be."

"I take enormous pride in your compliment, but it is very lonely to be me."

"I'm sorry. I suppose it *must* be lonely," said Mario. "But interesting times are coming—and so are interesting people. You'll see many of them in your lifetime."

"You know when and how I will die, don't you?"

"Don't ask."

"I was going to tell you never to impart that knowledge to me," said Leonardo. "It seems somehow"—he searched for the right word—"blasphemous."

"I know," said Mario. "Knowing all these things when I was part of a cloistered tour group was one thing. Knowing them while I am in your company is an awesome responsibility, even a frightening one."

"I appreciate that. I am doing my best not to ask you the thousands of questions that have occurred to me." The rain began again. "Can you run?"

"Don't worry about me," said the boy. "I promise I can keep up with you."

Leonardo began trotting, Mario fell into step beside him, and in another two minutes they had reached the artist's house. A note was tacked to the door, and Leonardo immediately pulled it off and read it. Before he was through his entire demeanor had changed, and he looked very worried.

"What is it?" asked Mario. "Has someone died?"

"Not yet," said Leonardo grimly. "It is from *il Moro*. He wants to know the color of the background in Cecilia's portrait, so that he can have a dress made for her that will match it." He shook his head irritably. "I know what will happen next," he continued. "He will ask me to change the color of her dress in the painting so that it is identical to the one he will present to her—as if I would ever have the background match the predominant color in the foreground. And of course it will fit differently, and the material will lay across her body differently. Of course I will refuse—my art comes first—and then he will almost certainly imprison me."

"Can he do that?"

"He is, for all practical purposes, the absolute ruler of Milan," answered Leonardo. "He can do anything. And it would save him the trouble of paying me all the money he owes me. I suppose I could live with that, but he might destroy the painting; that is the real tragedy of it."

"The background is white," said Mario, looking at the portrait. "Why not just tell him so?"

"The walnut board has been whitewashed prior to painting," said Leonardo. "I must decide upon a color, and it makes no difference, because he will order me to change her dress to match it." He paused, lost in thought. "Unless . . ."

"Unless?"

"Unless I can finish the painting before he returns in three weeks," said Leonardo. "If I present it to him to hang in the castle, Cecilia will never tolerate him taking it down and giving it back to me for another few months' of work—and he will neither imprison me nor destroy the painting if she approves of it. Yes, that's what I shall do!"

They entered the house, and Leonardo immediately walked to his studio, where Melody, who had been sleeping on a pile of rags, rose to greet him. He leaned down, petted her absently, and stared at *Lady with a Cat*.

"Background, background . . ." he murmured. Suddenly he turned to Mario. "Why am I agonizing over it? You know what color I chose! You can just tell me."

Mario shook his head. "I don't know what color you chose."

Leonardo looked crestfallen. "Then this portrait didn't survive?"

"I won't tell you if it still exists in the twenty-sixth century," said Mario, "but it survived long enough to be photographed and duplicated."

"Photographed?"

"Never mind. But yes, it survived you by many centuries."

"Then you *do* know the color."

"I already told you I don't."

"But you've *seen* it!"

"In my era we know how to preserve the most ancient paintings and artifacts, but for hundreds of years after the Renaissance people did not know the proper methods."

"I don't understand what you're saying," said Leonardo.

"Probably the paint began flaking a century or two after you painted it," explained Mario. "It's too beautiful to lose, so someone— no one knows who—tried to preserve it by painting over it. The background became black, but experts have determined that wasn't the original color."

"Black?" said Leonardo disgustedly. "They ruined my painting!"

"No," said Mario. "Much of it is untouched. But because of that, and other changes they made with the best of intentions, it wasn't conclusively proven to have been your work until almost four hundred years from now."

"I suppose I could sign it, as others do, though I consider it an egotistical affectation," mused Leonardo.

"It makes no difference," said Mario. "If a signature survived there would never have been any doubt that you were the artist, so either you won't sign it at all or you will sign it and someone will paint over your name."

"But it will survive four centuries, you say?" asked Leonardo, his expression brightening.

"At least."

"Then, for whatever reason, *il Moro* won't destroy it, and it will be worth the time and effort I have put into it." He studied the portrait, walked back and forth in front of it, looked at it from different angles. "It must be blue, of course," he said at last. "But what shade of blue? The same as Baldovinetti used some years back? No, he was limited by the nature of his paints. I can make the colors so much richer and subtler with my oils . . ."

Mario could see that Leonardo was lost in his thoughts, so he sat down on a chair and whistled for Melody to join him. She returned his whistle—a beautiful, lilting, other-worldly refrain—then walked over and jumped up onto his lap.

Leonardo saw the motion out of the corner of his eye and turned to look at the little animal.

"Yes!" he said excitedly. "Yes! It will work!"

"What are you talking about?" asked Mario.

"If I am replacing Prospero with Melody, then the sky will complement the blue of Melody's fur. A painting of 1490 will actually come to pass because of a color from 2523!" He smiled. "You know, someday they may invent an entire branch of literature devoted to such far-fetched suppositions."

Mario returned his smile. "They may indeed."

CHAPTER

NINE

Movement

Leonardo spent the next two hours lost in his notebooks, making endless annotations about the way he would mix the exact shade of blue he wanted; and while he was occupied with that, Mario thumbed through those notebooks that held his inventions.

The boy couldn't read his writing without a mirror, and none were handy, but it was clear from the sketches what Leonardo had in mind. There was a drawing of a bicycle, complete with a chain—a concept previously undreamed-of until the artist put pen to paper—but obviously he had never tried it out, because the pedals were longer than the wheels and would be stopped by the ground before the bike could get under way.

So what do I tell him? wondered Mario. *That bicycles do work, but that he's got a major flaw in his design? If I say that, he's sure to figure out what's wrong with the pedals, and then the bicycle will be invented hundreds of years before it should be. But if I tell him it doesn't work, he may abandon the principle of physically turning the wheels rather than using gravity or some external mechanism, before he finishes working on the drawings of his primitive tanks. So what do I say?*

The boy looked over at Leonardo, who was pacing up and down in front of the portrait, muttering to himself, jotting down an occasional note.

Everything interests him. He's like a moth drawn to the brightest flame. He's so taken by the painting that he may not even think to ask me about the notebooks.

"Yes," said Leonardo aloud, "it must be blue."

"I thought you'd decided on that hours ago," said Mario.

"Yes, yes," said the artist distractedly. "But originally I had planned to put Cecilia in an indoor setting." He looked around, picked up a paintbrush, dipped it in some oils, and quickly created a rectangular window in the upper right-hand corner of the painting. "I was going to have a window here, and the sun would fall upon her from this direction." He smiled. "So now the sun will not be forced to illuminate her narrowly through a window. The entire painting will be many shades brighter."

"And you will cover the outline of the window," said Mario.

"When I begin to paint the sky," agreed Leonardo. "I could wash it away right now, but why bother? I'll simply paint over it."

"I know."

Suddenly the artist was staring intently at him. "*How* do you know?"

"I've already told you that your background was covered with black paint," said Mario. "In the future, they'll use x-rays to determine the original color. They won't be able to find out, but they'll see that you had once placed a window in the upper right-hand corner."

"X-rays?" said Leonardo. "What are X-rays?"

"They're so far removed from any concept that exists today that I suppose I can tell you," said the boy. "You can't create them, paint them, or sketch them, so I don't see how you knowing about them can change the future."

"Well, then?"

"They are invisible rays, like beams of light that you cannot see, if that makes any sense to you. They can penetrate surfaces and see what lies beneath them."

"And can they see through the skin and bones of a man?" asked Leonardo.

A million uses and you instantly hit on the most important one. Aloud he said: "Yes, they can."

"Do men live forever in your era?"

"No," said Mario. "But most men live a full life span. Almost every injury and disease can be cured."

"It sounds like paradise."

"Not really," said Mario. "Nature keeps inventing new diseases, and we have other problems."

"That medicine cannot cure?"

"Medicine can't do much about hunger."

"Have farms become no more efficient?" asked Leonardo.

"They are far more efficient," said the boy.

"Then—?"

"There are less than half a billion people in *your* world," said Mario. "There will be twenty-eight billion in 2523 A.D. Even with undersea farms, the Earth simply cannot feed that many people. People have had to emigrate to other worlds, to spread our seed throughout the galaxy, to colonize worlds that are *not* overcrowded."

"Such concepts!" exclaimed Leonardo. "It is like a dream! And yet, with all that, you still know about me and my work. That is the most amazing thing of all. I have never thought of myself as a humble man, yet that is a humbling thought." And before Mario could reply, he added: "Move to your left."

"My left?"

"Your shadow has fallen on Melody, and I cannot see her true color."

"You were considering colors while we spoke?" asked Mario.

"I can easily do two things at once," replied the artist. "I can sometimes do three or four, if necessary. For example, even as I am considering how to reproduce Melody's color as the sun touches her from a certain angle, I am also determining how best to impart a sense of movement to her."

"Movement?" repeated Mario. "But this is a painting, not a—" He cut himself off. "It is a painting, so how can she move?"

"I must give her the *potential* of movement, not the kinetic," said Leonardo. "Come look at Cecilia and her horrible cat, and I will try to explain it to you."

Mario got up and walked over to the portrait. He ignored the hastily painted window and concentrated on the model and the animal.

"They *do* seem almost to be in motion," he said. "I never noticed that before, or rather it never registered, probably because almost every painter of the next thousand years will borrow and build on whatever it is you've done." He took a step closer. "But exactly what *have* you done?"

"Are you acquainted with the word *contrapossto*?" asked Leonardo.

"I never heard it before."

"Obviously the term did not survive," remarked Leonardo. "A pity. But at least the method did."

"So what is *contrapossto*?"

"It is the technique I have perfected—well, *developed*, anyway— to impart the illusion of movement to the painting," explained the artist.

"How does it work?"

"Observe Cecilia," said Leonardo. "She has been sitting, facing to her right. But something that you and I cannot see has approached from her left, and her head has turned to observe it. Do you see? I have captured an instant in time between when she becomes aware of this unknown *thing* to her left and when she turns her full body to face it squarely."

"Yes," said Mario. "I can see that now."

"But there is more to it than that, which is why I must study Melody still further. The cat on her lap has been facing to the right as well, and now, suddenly startled, it too is watching the approaching *something*. Its every movement reflects Cecilia's own. The two figures complement each other, for if only Cecilia had known there was something of interest to her left, you could reasonably assume that the cat, with its superior senses, was dead."

"That makes sense," agreed Mario.

"Now, Melody has a longer body than Prospero. She is built more along the lines of a ferret, so I must find out exactly how much of her would turn when she first becomes aware that something is off to her left." He paused. "I wish I had seen a member of her species dissected so that I could study its musculature, but that of course is out of the question."

"Do you dissect many animals?"

"I participate in the dissection of dead dogs and horses and cats and, especially, birds, just as I participate in the dissection of dead men and women. How else can an artist learn everything he must know about the way humans are made, the way they move and the way they cannot move?"

"Do all the major artists do the same?"

"There are those who seem totally intuitive, but I think it is just that subconscious you mentioned working while they are not aware of it. You do not really have to dissect a man to know that his elbow only bends in one direction or that his ears do not prick up like a horse or hang down like a dog's."

"And yet you have filled many of these notebooks with detailed drawings of the human body," said Mario.

"Perhaps I don't trust my subconscious," said Leonardo. "Or perhaps I simply haven't the patience to wait upon it. I can wait for inspiration, or I can logically and scientifically determine exactly how to impart a sense of movement to a painting. I prefer the second method. I prefer logic to inspiration, and it has the added advantage that if it works once and I can codify it, it will work every time."

"I'm not arguing with you," replied the boy. "I am just trying to learn what I can from you while I'm here and have the opportunity."

"That's reasonable," said Leonardo. "I'm trying to do the same with Melody while *she* is here." He paused. "Perhaps I should call it *Lady with a Singer*."

"People will wonder where the madrigal singer is," said Mario.

"You have a point," agreed the artist. He consider the portrait, then looked down at Melody and back at the painting. "It shall be *Lady with an Alien*."

Omygod! thought the boy. *You're not supposed to know about aliens! No one in this era is. Will that be enough to change the future?*

Belief

Mario was being shaken awake. He muttered something unintelligible and rolled over. A firm hand grasped his shoulder and shook him again.

"What is it?" he said, keeping his eyes closed.

"Come, my young friend," said Leonardo's voice. "It is morning."

"Morning?" said Mario, sitting up and rubbing his eyes. "But I was just watching you mix paints in the studio."

"You fell asleep. At one point you woke up, and I directed you to my apprentice's room, which is where you are. He is visiting his mother in Paris, so his room is your room until he returns."

"I thought he'd sleep on a straw mattress in the attic," said the boy. "At least that's what the history books say about apprentices in the Renaissance."

"My other apprentices do sleep in the attic," acknowledged the artist. "But this one's parents are wealthy enough to pay me for his room."

"Have you slept at all?" asked Mario, swinging his legs onto the floor.

"A few hours," said Leonardo. "It's all that I need, and I resent giving up even that much time, time during which I could be working or thinking—especially when my freedom may be at stake." He watched Mario stretch and try to clear his mind. "Are you hungry?"

The boy considered the question, and realized that he was indeed very hungry. "Yes."

"Good. I often have breakfast with a friend, a poet named Bernardo. I will not tell him the truth about you, but he can be trusted not to spread gossip, so you may feel free to speak to him instead of pretending to be a mute."

"*That's* a relief," said Mario, standing up. He rinsed his face, dried it, stretched again, and then followed Leonardo out the door and into the street, shading his eyes from the morning sun.

"There is no sign of rain today, so you will not need any protection against the weather."

"Are we going to your friend's house?"

Leonardo looked amused. "He is an even worse cook than I am. No, we will be meeting him at a local *taverna*."

"I have no money to pay for my meal."

"They do not charge me," replied Leonardo. "I do them the occasional favor, and they feed me the occasional meal." He turned to the boy. "Do tarot cards exist in the twenty-sixth century?"

"Yes."

The artist sighed. "I had hoped they would just be a passing fancy, soon forgotten."

"What do tarot cards have to do with anything?"

"The owner of the *taverna* sells them," explained Leonardo. "I have done the preliminary sketches for a number of cards. Then lesser artists do the actual painting."

"Like inkers and colorists in comic art," suggested the boy.

"Humorous art? I do not understand."

"It's too difficult to explain. Anyway, now I know what you're talking about."

As they walked, Leonardo pointed out some sights they had missed the previous day due to the rain, and before long they arrived at their destination.

Maybe the rain washed the city clean, thought Mario, *but somehow it doesn't look quite as filthy and foreboding today. Or am I just getting used to it?*

A short man, burly without being fat, his eyebrows bushy, the hair atop his head thinning, was waiting for them just outside the front door.

"Greetings, my friend," he said, then turned to Mario. "And who is this?"

"This is my cousin Mario, who is visiting from a distant land," said Leonardo. "And Mario, this is the finest poet in Milan, Bernardo Bellincioni."

"He only says that because I wrote nice things about his last painting," said Bernardo with a smile. "If I don't like his next one, he will doubtless introduce me as the worst poet in Milan."

"And if you don't like my next painting, it will be true," said Leonardo.

Bernardo laughed and turned to Mario. "He is better with his paintbrush than Botticelli, he is better with science than any lecturer in the university, and as you can see he is better with words than I am.

I think the rest of the world can be thankful that he was never interested in the art of war."

"It is a science, not an art," said Leonardo, as he entered the *taverna*, followed by Mario and Bernardo. Bernardo found a small empty table in one corner and the three of them sat down. The owner immediately brought them wine, greeted Leonardo like a brother, gently reminded him that he hadn't sketched a new tarot card in almost two months, and then asked each of them what they wanted to eat.

"The usual," said Leonardo, and the owner vanished into the kitchen, returning a moment later with eggs, fruit, and bread.

"So, Mario," said Bernardo as the owner left again, "have you been enjoying yourself in Milan?"

"Very much," replied Mario, uncomfortably conscious of his accent and using as few words as possible.

"Has he shown you the Cathedral yet?"

"We were going to see it yesterday, but it rained," interjected Leonardo.

"That was just God castigating you for cutting open corpses and drawing pictures of their innards," said Bernardo jokingly.

"God gave me a brain," replied Leonardo. "It would be a sin not to use it."

"He gave Eve an appetite and look what happened," said the poet with a chuckle.

Leonardo turned to Mario. "Pay no attention," he said. "We have this discussion almost every day. Once it's over, we can get on to important things."

"So today God is not important?" said Bernardo teasingly.

"He has not struck you mute yet, so obviously He is not paying attention to our conversion," replied the artist.

A customer passed near the table, and Bernardo instantly fell silent until he was out of earshot, then looked to make sure no one else was listening.

"We can tease each other," he said softly to Mario, "but there are many who take a dim view of such things, as they do of your cousin."

"But why?" asked Mario. "There is nothing offensive in his paintings."

"That is a matter of some debate," said the poet.

"I do not paint halos above the saints," explained Leonardo.

"And this upsets some in positions of power," added Bernardo. He looked amused. "Fortunately, he has a protector in *il Moro*."

For the moment anyway, thought Mario. He took a bite of his bread, prepared to be disappointed, and was surprised to find that it tasted quite good. More to the point, it tasted fresh, which was something he hadn't experienced before. He decided he liked it.

"The day I see a halo I'll paint it," said Leonardo. "Until then I shall paint the real world as I observe it."

"They also object to his dissection of human corpses."

"God made us different from the animals!" snapped Leonardo. "I will not pretend I am as stupid as a cow just to make someone else happy!" The sound of his voice caused heads to turn, and the artist waited until everyone had gone back to eating. "It is ridiculous. I do not have to paint halos or remain ignorant to prove that I believe in the Almighty. It might even be sacrilegious."

"Sacrilegious in what way?"

"If God created everything for a purpose, what did He create the human brain for, if not to inquire after everything?"

"Then He created religion to hold it in check," said Bernardo, looking enormously pleased with himself.

"*Now* which of us is the greater sinner?" asked Leonardo, returning his friend's smile.

"Then perhaps you should teach me to write backwards too," suggested Bernardo.

"Why?" asked Mario, curious in spite of himself.

"We hope the Inquisition will be confined to Spain," said Bernardo. "But this is the same church in Milan. Sometimes it is not a bad idea to put one's thoughts down in a script that no one can read." He looked around to make sure he couldn't be overheard. "Especially the Inquisitors."

"That is not why I write in that manner," said Leonardo.

"I know," said Bernardo. "You write like that because you are self-taught and left-handed. But I suspect there is a valid reason why you have never trained yourself to write in the normal fashion. Certainly it would be no great challenge for a man of your gifts."

Leonardo seemed about to argue, then shrugged and took a bite of his meal instead. Bernardo did the same, and Mario got the distinct impression that the morning's religious banter was done, that it had perhaps gotten a little more heated than usual.

"The Inquisition will not come to Italy," said Leonardo after he washed down his food with some of his wine.

"I hope you're right," said Bernardo. "I just wish that when people were slaughtered, it wasn't always in the name of God."

"It isn't," said Leonardo. "Sometimes people are slaughtered in the name of conquest."

"True," acknowledged Bernardo.

"And sometimes they are slaughtered in the name of justice."

"Oh?" said Bernardo. "When and where did this happen?"

"Transylvania."

"Him?" said Bernardo. "He was crazy!"

"There are those who say he wasn't." Leonardo turned to Mario. "I am referring to Count Vlad Dracule of Transylvania, better known as Vlad the Impaler. In the name of justice, he put more than one hundred thousand men and women to death. His favorite method of execution was to impale his still-living victims on stakes."

"He was a madman," insisted Bernardo. "Mark my words—fifty years from now he will be totally forgotten. No one will even know that such a monster existed."

"Perhaps," said Leonardo noncommittally. "But he served his purpose."

"Purpose?" Bernardo practically shouted. "What possible purpose could be served by killing most of his country's population?"

"The Black Plague was advancing toward the heart of Europe," replied the artist. "It came to an end in Transylvania, for there was no one left alive to carry it across the border to neighboring countries."

"My God!" exclaimed Bernardo. "The man's not just a painter and an inventor and a poet, but now he's an historian and a philosopher as well."

"I'm an excellent singer too," said Leonardo.

"Is there anything you do *not* excel in, my friend?" said Bernardo.

Leonardo smiled. "Modesty," he replied.

ELEVEN

Technique

After they had finished eating, Bernardo expressed a desire to see Cecilia's portrait.

"It's not done yet," replied Leonardo cautiously.

"That's never stopped you from showing off before," said Bernardo.

"I'm making some changes to it," said Leonardo. "I'd really rather not have you see it until they're done."

"Nonsense!" scoffed Bernardo. "If I like it, I'll publish a sonnet proclaiming its virtues. You always need money. Think of how much you can sell it for with my help."

"It's already sold."

"But not paid for, if I know *il Moro*," said Bernardo with a chuckle.

"You know *il Moro*," conceded the artist.

"Anyway, what are we waiting for?" said Bernardo. "Let's stop by your house and let me take a look at it."

"I'm changing the background right now," protested Leonardo.

"You're drinking wine right now," shot back the poet.

"Perhaps tomorrow."

"I know how slowly and carefully you work," persisted Bernardo. "It won't look any different tomorrow than today."

"This time you are mistaken," said Leonardo. "I must finish it before *il Moro* returns home."

"So he finally got tired of your inability to complete a project remotely on schedule?" said Bernardo with an amused smile. "You can always hide in my house."

"I think it's serious this time."

"I'm sorry to hear it, my friend. But I'd still like to see it. What are you hiding?"

"Nothing," said Leonardo, defeated. "We will go look at the painting. But let me send my cousin ahead to make the studio more presentable. It was in total disarray when we left."

"That never bothered you before."

"Well, it bothers me today. Run along, Mario, and tidy things up. We'll join you in a few minutes."

Oh, my gosh! thought the boy. *I forgot all about Melody! He wants me to hide her before Bernardo gets there!*

"Yes, Leonardo," he said, getting to his feet and hurrying out of the taverna.

"A very nice young man," said Bernardo. "I can't place his accent, though. It's definitely not French or English. Where does he come from?"

Let me think. Where will you never go, and who are you least likely to have met?

"Western Africa," said Leonardo at last. "His parents are originally from Florence, but he has spent so much time with the natives that our own tongue is almost a second language to him."

"Well, that certainly explains it," said Bernardo, obviously satisfied.

How easy that was, thought Leonardo. *Perhaps along with essays I should consider writing fanciful tales as the English have done. I must remember to make a note of that when I get home.*

The artist engaged his friend in idle chatter for another few minutes, then got to his feet and began walking very slowly toward his house.

"What is the name of this painting?" asked the poet as they neared their destination.

Have I eliminated all trace of the cat yet? thought Leonardo. *I can't remember. Better not to say anything.* Aloud he replied: "I haven't decided yet."

Mario, who had been watching from a window as they approached, opened the door and stepped outside to greet them.

"Did you clean things up a little?" asked Leonardo.

"I got the worst of it put away," answered the boy.

They exchanged knowing looks, and Leonardo entered the house. "Come to the studio, Bernardo, and tell me everything I've done wrong." Suddenly he smiled. "And I insist that you do so in rhyming couplets."

"An unfinished painting deserves an unwritten poem," shot back Bernardo. "Now let me see this masterpiece."

They walked into the studio, and Bernardo stopped before the portrait, staring transfixed at it.

"If you finish it as well as you have started it," said the poet at last, "you will indeed have outdone yourself. This is an exemplary use of *chiaroscuro*."

"Excuse me," interrupted Mario, "but that is a word I am not familiar with."

"*Chiaroscuro?*" repeated Bernardo. "It is a technique that defines forms through the contrasts of light and darkness. You see the contrast of her delicate fingers with the white fur of the cat, and the cat actually helps the eye see all the lines of her arm, just as the black necklace clearly defines her neck." He turned to Leonardo. "I see patches of blue, as if you are trying to determine the proper color for the sky. Will she be seen to be outside, then?"

"Yes," answered Leonardo. "Originally I had planned to put her in her own parlor, but . . ."

"But *il Moro* meddled?" suggested Bernardo.

The artist nodded his head. "Yes. And no one meddles with my art."

"Well, if he was ever going to meddle with this one, now is the right time."

"I don't understand," said Mario.

"He hasn't brought the *sfumato* to completion," answered the poet.

"My ignorance is showing again," said Mario. "What is *sfumato?*"

"Another technique your cousin has perfected," said Bernardo.

"*Sfumato* is the means by which I try to make my paintings indistinguishable from the real world," explained Leonardo. "I make my underpainting by adding white tints and black tones to pure colors."

"How does that work?" asked Mario.

"I dilute my oil paints, then layer transparent glazes and add mixtures of pure colors with touches of black to enhance the sense of depth. Finally I apply lighter shades over the darker colors to give the finished work a sense of"—he searched for the proper word— "luminosity."

"Luminosity?" repeated Mario, puzzled.

"The glow of life, just as your own flesh glows with life and a corpse's does not," replied Leonardo. A self-deprecating smile crossed his face. "At least that is the theory."

"And these techniques are all based on science, like the others you described to me?"

"Certainly," said the artist. "Many are my own creations. Some I have worked out with my friend Luca Pacioli, a great mathematician. And for some I have simply borrowed what others have done and built upon it. But it is *all* based on science."

"Now if we could just convince him to work on larger boards," said Bernardo, staring at the walnut panel that held the painting.

"It is large enough for my purposes," answered Leonardo.

I was so taken by its beauty that I hardly noticed before, thought Mario, *but it's not even two feet by eighteen inches. I wonder what size the* Mona Lisa *will be?*

"There is just one thing lacking," said Bernardo, still studying the painting.

"Besides the background, you mean?" replied the artist sardonically.

"It's the cat."

"What about the cat?"

"There's something wrong," said Bernardo. "Oh, it's an accurate

rendition, there's no question of that. But there is something . . . well
. . . lacking. I get the distinct impression that you don't care for that
animal, indeed that you dislike it."

"Is it that easy to tell?" said Leonardo.

"Yes, it is," said the poet. "If I were you, I would eliminate it from
the painting altogether. Replace it with another animal, or perhaps a
bouquet of flowers."

"An excellent suggestion, my friend," said Leonardo. "I promise
that I shall do just that."

"Then when it is shown, I will be able to tell all Milan that I
had something to do with one of the Master's paintings!" bragged
Bernardo. "I suppose I will have to let you write a few lines of one of
my sonnets in exchange."

"Perhaps," said Leonardo, his mind racing. *Did we feed Melody
before we left or not? And if not, how soon before she begins that
other-worldly singing?* "I am glad you like what I have done thus far,
my old friend. And now you must excuse me while I go back to work
and consider what to put in the cat's place."

"Certainly," said Bernardo, looking incredibly pleased with himself. "And if you need any further advice, don't hesitate to ask."

He walked to the front door, let himself out, and began walking
away. He had been out of earshot for less than a minute when Melody
broke into song to remind them that someone had forgotten to feed
the pet.

Inventions

"I have kept my end of the bargain, at the possible cost of my freedom," announced Leonardo. "It is time you began keeping yours."

"All right," replied Mario. "I'll do so, within the limitations we agreed on."

"Fair enough," said the artist. He walked to a pile of notebooks, looked through them, settled on a pair, and, rather than handing them to Mario, laid them out on a table. "Let us begin with this one."

He thumbed through the pages until he came to some sketches of a flying man, with feathered, artificial wings attached to his arms.

"I am genuinely sorry to tell you this," said the boy, "but it won't work."

"But it *must!*" insisted Leonardo. "Melody is from another world. Don't tell me you walked there!"

"No, we didn't walk there," said Mario. "I never said that humans will not master the art of flying—but they will not fly in the way that you have illustrated."

"I have studied the birds all my life," said Leonardo, puzzled. "What other way is there?"

"All I can tell you is that it exists."

"Will I discover the method you use?"

"You know I can't answer that."

"Now that I know that men will fly, I will never stop trying to find out how," promised the artist.

Mario remained silent, afraid that if he made any answer at all, he would reveal more than he should. When Leonardo realized that the boy was not going to expand upon what he had said, he hastily paged through the notebook until he came to the sketch of a bulky parachute.

"And this?" he said.

"I don't think it will work quite as you have drawn it," said Mario. "It is too large and too awkward, and you should use lighter materials; but you're on the right track. It will be called a parachute when it is perfected."

"A parachute," Leonardo repeated, mouthing the word carefully. A look of immense relief spread across his face.

"Thank God! For a moment I was afraid that nothing I had imagined would work."

"This will work."

Leonardo stared thoughtfully at the sketch, then looked up at Mario. "Men will fly," he said at last.

"I already told you that."

"You needn't have told me. Just telling me that this invention works is enough, for how can it work if men cannot fly high above the ground and then release it? If you were to carry it to a mountaintop and then leap off with it, the winds would likely buffet you against the side of the mountain, killing you. So if the parachute will be used in the future, it will be used by men who fly."

Mario smiled. "You're very perceptive."

"Not as perceptive as I wish," said Leonardo, "for there is clearly a problem here. Birds have hollow bones and a musculature designed for flight. Even if my artificial wings work, they will barely lift a man into the air; they will certainly not lift a parachute."

"True."

"But if my wings don't work, how will men be able to get aloft?"

Mario didn't answer.

"It is enough to know that they will do so," continued Leonardo. "All problems are capable of solution. Eventually I will solve this one." He shot a quick look at the boy, but Mario kept his face expressionless. "So much for wings." The artist picked up the other book, rifled through the pages until he came to the sketches he wanted, and showed them to the boy. "Will this machine work?"

"Not quite," said Mario.

"What does that mean?"

"What you've drawn is an engine of war that will someday be known as a tank," said Mario, staring at the sketches. "The coming centuries will see numerous improvements, but the basic idea will remain unchanged: a machine that is capable of enormous destruction to the enemy while at the same time protecting the men who ride inside it."

"Note the blades that come out the sides," said Leonardo. "As the machine goes through the enemy lines, those who do not turn and flee will be dismembered."

"It's a pretty brutal machine for a man who cherishes life," noted the boy.

"I only paint saints," said Leonardo. "I do not pretend to be one." He sighed deeply. "I try to be a good man and to live by certain ethical principles; but I must eat, and I must pay for my paints and my raw materials, and I must feed my apprentices. The man who pays me is Ludovico Sforza, and he tolerates my painting and my gentler inventions only so long as I provide him with weapons of war."

"Don't you find a certain contradiction in that?" asked Mario.

"These engines of destruction are simply concepts," explained Leonardo. "I wish to know if they work, of course, because I am curious to know if I have discovered the proper principles; but I draw them primarily to keep *il Moro* happy. Every time he asks me to build a prototype, I explain that I am still perfecting it, and thus far he has been willing to wait."

"How long can you get away with that?" asked the boy. "Have you produced anything for him?"

"Of course I have," answered Leonardo. "The man is no fool." He opened another sketchbook and turned to a particular illustration. "Do you see this?"

"It's a bridge," said Mario, unimpressed.

"True," agreed the artist. "But it is a very special bridge."

"In what way?"

"It is a *movable* bridge. Sforza can have his men place it over a river, march or ride across the water, and then take it with him to the next river."

"That's a pretty neat idea," admitted the boy.

"Child's play."

Mario smiled. "I thought you were kidding when you said you weren't very good at modesty."

"It was less of a joke than it should be," said the artist. "If I didn't spend so much time convincing *il Moro* and his court that I am a genius, I couldn't live as one; and sometimes I forget that I do not have to impress everybody." He turned back to the page with the primitive tank on it. "You said this worked in principle but not in practice?"

"That's right."

"I realize that you cannot tell me how to make it work, but can you at least tell me where it fails to work?"

"I'm going to use a term you won't understand," said Mario. "The problem is that you don't know how to create differential gears."

"Differ—?" began Leonardo, trying to mouth the word.

"What I'm saying is that the machine will protect the men inside it and the blades are as deadly as you think, but it won't be able to move on level ground."

"But it has wheels, and men inside to make the wheels turn," protested Leonardo.

"They won't be able to turn the wheels," said Mario.

"They *will!*" insisted Leonardo.

"I'm not going to argue it," said Mario. "You're a lot smarter than I am, and for all I know, you're trying to get me to tell you something you shouldn't know—or at least something that you should discover or figure out without my help."

Leonardo stared at the sketch again. "But *why* won't they turn?" he muttered, more to himself than to the boy.

"You've created the basic notion of a tank," said Mario. "In centuries to come men will build more than a million of them. They will be capable of greater speed and more destruction than even you can imagine, and it will all come from your concept. Isn't that enough?"

"Falling short of perfection is never enough," said Leonardo unhappily.

"It'll have to do."

Leonardo thumbed through the notebooks. "I have designed a machine of perpetual motion," he began.

"It won't work."

"But you haven't even looked at the drawings!" complained Leonardo. "Or have you examined them in the future?"

"No, I haven't."

"Then how can you judge my machine?" demanded the artist, trying to control his anger.

"To have a machine of perpetual motion, you must power it with a source of perpetual energy," answered Mario. "If you power it with animals, sooner or later they will tire or die. Power it with water and sooner or later the water will evaporate. Power it with fire and sooner or later you will run out of fuel and the fire will go out. You know nothing of solar power, but sooner or later night falls. And by definition a perpetual motion machine can *never* stop."

"This is very depressing," said Leonardo unhappily. He shoved a notebook at Mario. "Is there *anything* in there that will work?"

The boy opened the book and thumbed through it. "Yes," he said,

"I see a number of things that will either work right now or will work with minimal changes."

"What are they?" asked Leonardo eagerly.

"The water wheel with the cups attached," said the boy. "They'll still be using that hundreds of years from now." He turned another page. "The siphon will work, either as you've drawn it or with a minor improvement or two. And this machine—it looks like it's made for dredging. You're definitely on the right track with it."

Mario spent the next half hour going through another half dozen notebooks, pointing out those inventions that he thought were based on sound reasoning.

"Thank you," said Leonardo when they were done. "You've made me feel like not all my work has been wasted."

"None of it has been," answered the boy. "We learn from people's mistakes as much as from their successes."

"Can I make you something to eat before I go back to work on Cecilia's portrait?"

"No, thanks," said Mario. "I thought I'd go for a little walk and get some fresh air."

"Is it that stuffy in here?"

"No—but fresh air is something new to me. I kind of enjoyed it."

"Even with the smells you complained about?"

"If I'm going to be here for another two weeks, I might as well get used to them." *Besides, I find the smell of freshly cooked bread intriguing. I was kind of hoping to pass by a bakery.*

"Don't stray too far," said Leonardo. "Not everyone is as friendly as Bernardo."

"I'll be careful," said Mario, walking to the front door and stepping outside.

All right, he thought. *A town and a time that could produce men like Leonardo and Bernardo can't be all bad. Maybe it's time I started looking beneath the grime.*

He set off on his solo tour of the city. It was just as dirty and impoverished as before, but this time he was looking for virtues rather than faults, and he was pretty sure he'd find some.

Sacrifice

"I wish I knew which of my oil mixtures would last the longest," remarked Leonardo, as he took a break from the painting. "I try something different each time. So many of the ancient paintings, or even those from the last century, have decayed through age, or even sunlight."

"Many of yours will last," said Mario, who had just returned from an invigorating walk past the buildings that would *not* survive the century but which he found all the more fascinating because of their uniqueness. "A few will be preserved by methods that I'm not expert enough to describe even if I were permitted to."

"And some will not?"

"Some will not."

The artist sighed. "A thousand years is a long time, longer than I have any right to hope for. It is enough that they will outlive me."

"*That* I can guarantee," said the boy.

"This is a good painting," said Leonardo, indicating the portrait of Cecilia. "A fine painting. But I feel I have greater work within me, that there will come a day when I produce a painting of such quality that I will almost want to disown this one."

"This is a beautiful painting," replied Mario. "Why would you want to disown it?"

"Because, as I said . . ." began Leonardo.

"If you want me to tell you whether or not you will produce works of more renown, you know I can't do that."

"It is so frustrating!" said Leonardo. "I want to know if I am taking my art in the right direction. You know the answer. It would be so simple to just say yes or no."

"You know I can't," said Mario. "Use that brain of yours to figure it out."

Leonardo glared at him for a moment and then did just what the boy suggested. After a moment he relaxed and smiled. "Thank you, my young friend. That was all the hint I needed." He pointed to the portrait. "If that was my greatest contribution to the world of art, tours from your distant age would not bother to come back and observe me. They would spend their time studying Botticelli and Donatello."

"You are content now?"

"I am content."

"I'm glad that's over with," said Mario.

"I think I shall relax for a few hours before returning to the painting."

"That's a question I've been meaning to ask. How *do* you relax?"

"I write, I read, I draw, I walk through the streets of Milan as you just did and let my mind wander. Why? Do the artists of your era have a specific way of relaxing?"

The boy shook his head. "No. I was just thinking of a Spanish painter who will be born almost halfway between your era and mine. His name will be Picasso. He will be a very prolific artist, producing hundreds of paintings, perhaps thousands. When someone asks him what he does for a hobby, he will reply that he paints. When asked how he relaxes, he will give the same answer." He paused thoughtfully. "I don't know if that's love or dedication or both."

"Or perhaps madness."

"Why do you think so?" asked Mario.

"If you know of him five centuries after his birth and death, he must have been a fine painter," said Leonardo. "But I do not understand a man who can be satisfied with only one area of expertise."

"Not every painter is also a mathematician and a scientist," replied Mario. "In fact, hardly any are."

"I am not limited to that," said Leonardo proudly. He walked to another room and returned a moment later with a device that looked like the life-sized silver outline of a horse's head, strung with wires.

"What is that?" asked the boy.

"When I first arrived in Milan, I was invited to a party at Ludovico Sforza's. He too was impressed by my many talents, and challenged me to prove that I could sing too. I told him to give me until his next gathering, and I would not only sing but accompany myself on the lute. He told me to borrow a lute from one of his court musicians, but I told him that I preferred my own. That evening I went home and began constructing this instrument, shaped like the head of *il Moro's* favorite horse."

Leonardo ran his fingers over the strings, and a lovely chord filled the room, eliciting a musical response from Melody. "I brought it with me to his next party, and it was so well received that I have been asked to bring it to every party he has given since then." He looked down at Melody.

"You wish to sing to your friend, do you?" he said, playing a simple tune. Melody responded instantly, matching it note for note, and looked puzzled that the lute did not speak to her again. "We could do this all day, and I would still not understand what she is saying," said Leonardo, putting the silver instrument down on the floor. "Or what my lute is saying either."

Melody immediately approached the lute, sniffed at it, rubbed against it, and when it made no further sound, eventually lost interest in it.

Leonardo was about to speak again when a messenger, a boy about Mario's age, pounded on the door. Leonardo opened it and accepted a rolled-up piece of paper. He took it back inside the house, opened it up, and read it.

"It is just as well I stopped painting when I did," he announced.

"What is it?" asked Mario. "Not bad news, I hope."

"Good news," answered Leonardo. "I have a standing request with Ospedale Maggiore to notify me whenever they will be dissecting a fresh corpse. They will be doing so shortly." He paused, then added: "Occasionally they even allow me to participate."

"It sounds disgusting."

"One gets used to it," replied Leonardo. "And how else am I to learn the secrets of the human body if I cannot study the musculature? You have seen my notebooks, and you heard Bernardo. You know this is something I have done before and will continue to do."

"I know," said the boy. "It's just that the thought of dissecting dead people makes me feel . . ." He searched for the right word but couldn't find it.

"You can stay here," said the artist. "I'll only be an hour or two."

"No," said Mario, steeling himself for the experience to come. "I'll go with you—provided I don't have to cut or touch anything."

"I promise you will do nothing but observe."

"All right," said Mario, "let's go."

"Would you care to eat first?"

"Good God, no!" said the boy. "This is going to be upsetting enough as it is."

Leonardo smiled. "We will eat on the way home. Let's go."

He went to the door, and a moment later they were walking down the paved streets of Milan.

"Where exactly is this body being kept?" asked Mario.

"At Ospedale del Brolo, a division of the Ospedale Maggiore hospital," answered Leonardo. He glanced at the boy. "Don't look so ill. They never invite me if the person died of a disease."

"I'm probably vaccinated for every disease known to the Renaissance," said Mario.

"Vaccinated?" repeated Leonardo, suddenly interested. "What does that mean?"

Damn! thought the boy. *I did it again!* Finally he shrugged and said, "Protected."

"As with holy water?" asked Leonardo, studying him carefully.

"Just protected."

"We will let the subject drop; but later today, while I am painting,

I want you to tell me of some of the accomplishments of the medical sciences. I am no doctor, and I can make no use of anything you tell me. Besides, I am sure most of it will be indistinguishable from magic to me. But I would like to hear of it anyway."

The boy nodded his agreement. "I'll tell you what I think is safe, which is to say what I think you can't change by knowing in advance what will happen."

"That is all I ask."

"No, it isn't," said Mario with a smile. "But it is all you're going to get."

Leonardo laughed, threw an arm around the boy's shoulders, and continued walking to the Ospedale del Brolo.

When they arrived they were ushered into a stone chamber where the body of a young woman lay on a long table. Her skull had been crushed, either from the kick of a horse or perhaps a fall, and for the next two hours her body was dissected, the skin peeled back, the internal organs removed, the skeleton examined. Throughout it all Leonardo made sketch after sketch of what he saw.

Finally they were done, and Leonardo walked over to Mario, who had stood as far from the body as possible and had spent most of the time with his eyes shut.

"We can leave now," said the artist.

"Good," said the boy, feeling momentarily dizzy as he took his first few steps. When they emerged into the open, he took a number of deep breaths, reveling in the fresh air.

"Fascinating, was it not?" said Leonardo.

"It was ghoulish."

"One makes sacrifices for one's art."

"How does cutting up a dead woman constitute a sacrifice?" asked Mario, feeling stronger with each step he put between himself and the stone chamber.

"A poet sacrifices the pleasure of reading poetry, for once he becomes a poet, he must read everything with an analytical eye; he must learn from both the failures and the successes of his rivals. The hunter cannot appreciate the beauty of his prey but must study its habits and learn its weaknesses." He paused. "But an artist not only loses the ability to uncritically appreciate works of art, but also he must learn everything possible about how to create believable works of art himself. And one of the things he sacrifices is a sense of horror and disgust at anything that will aid his art. I assure you that as a small boy I did not envision a lifetime of cutting open corpses and drawing what I found beneath their skins."

"When you put it that way, I guess it *is* a sacrifice after all," admitted the boy.

"It is," said Leonardo. "From the day that you truly dedicate yourself to art, your only pleasure comes from doing it well, not from seeing it well done." A wistful expression crossed his face. "It is the one thing I regret about my choice of professions."

Mathematics

As Leonardo and Mario were returning from Ospedale del Brola, they were greeted by a small, wiry, white-haired man who seemed to have dressed by grabbing the nearest available pieces of clothing with no effort to match the colors or styles.

"You have been hiding from me, Leonardo," rasped the man gruffly. "Were we not supposed to be calculating the orbits of the celestial bodies?" He turned to Mario. "He is quite the brilliant thinker, your friend Leonardo. He can theorize better than any man I know. But give him four small sums to add together, and he'll be wrong more often than not." He smiled triumphantly. "That's why he needs me."

Leonardo seemed vastly amused. "Mario, meet Luca Pacioli, my friend and mentor, who never misses an opportunity to remind people—even people he doesn't know—that he is a better mathematician than I am."

Luca stared intently at the boy. "Got you adding his sums, has he?"

"Not yet," answered Mario.

"Good. Come to my house and I'll teach you properly. Or are you another one of his young artists?"

"He is a distant cousin, visiting for the fortnight," interjected Leonardo.

"Well, come on over anyway," said Luca, "and at least you won't starve to death. I know his apprentices are all on holiday, and I've tasted his cooking."

Mario spotted the twinkle in the old man's eye and decided that he probably teased Leonardo like this all the time.

I haven't met anyone here I haven't liked and who I don't find interesting, he thought. *I wish I could say that about my own era.*

"I shouldn't say this in front of him," said Leonardo confidentially, "but he really is the finest mathematician in Milan."

"Perhaps in all the world," added Luca. "At the very least, in all of Italy."

"I am honored to meet you, sir," said Mario.

"As well you should be," growled Luca, but now Mario saw that this was simply the old man's notion of humor.

"Where are you going, Luca?" asked Leonardo. "This is early in the day for you. Lately you've been up half the night studying the heavenly bodies."

"I got thirsty, and I realized I had run out of wine. Come with me and I will buy you each a flagon—not that you deserve it."

"We were about to stop for a meal," replied Leonardo. "We'll be happy to join you, and you can still pay for the drinks."

"I prefer water, but I'll be happy to come," said Mario.

"Water?" repeated Luca, making a face. "The last two men I knew who liked water both died horribly. Trust me, boy, wine's healthier."

He's probably right, thought Mario. The water's doubtless crawling with all kinds of bacteria. At least the alcohol kills the germs.

"There is a *taverna* here and one around the corner," said Leonardo. "Which do you prefer?"

"My keen mathematical mind tells me this one is closer," said Luca, turning and walking through the doorway, then leading the way to a table.

The three of them sat down. Mario looked for a menu, couldn't find one, and decided that, like the prior *taverna* he'd been to, they would take what was available or go hungry, that selections of food items was probably still a century or two away. Still, his companions didn't seem concerned, and he hadn't had a bad meal since coming back to Milan in search of Melody, so he decided not to worry about it.

"How has your work been going, Luca?" asked Leonardo as the proprietor came by with a pitcher of wine and three wooden cups.

"If you would come over more often, you wouldn't have to ask," replied the mathematician.

"Fine," said Leonardo, smiling. "I apologize for bothering you with a trivial question. The subject is closed."

"Like hell it is!" snapped Luca. "I am calculating the motions of Mars and Venus, to better help that Columbus fellow guide his ships by night—and I'm doing it a damned sight better than Regiomontanus did!"

"Regiomontanus?" repeated Mario.

"The man just published a book called *Table of Directions,* which is a damned silly name for a book about spherical astronomy," said Luca, and this time he seemed genuinely grumpy. "If Columbus pays any attention to it, he's likely to wind up on the coast of Africa."

"As you can see, I get my modesty from Luca," said Leonardo with a grin.

"The man's simply wrong!" snapped Luca, pounding the table with a fist. "*You* know the Earth isn't the center of the universe. *I* know it's not. I simply cannot figure out why these so-called astronomers don't know it."

"Give them time," said Mario, trying to remember when Copernicus was born. He knew that the astronomer was part of the Renaissance, but he couldn't remember the dates. Finally he shrugged. Obviously he either hadn't been born yet or at least hadn't announced his findings.

"Amateurs all," complained Luca. "The science of mathematics is central to the understanding of everything, and yet they all disdain it."

"How is it central to painting?" asked Mario. "Leonardo has explained how he imparts a sense of movement to his art, but what does math have to do with it?"

"Perspective, proportion, angles of observation, these are *all* dependent on mathematics," said Luca. "Let me give you a simple example. How many heads tall is a man?"

"I have no idea," answered Mario, who felt simultaneously out of his depth and pleased that the adults in this era were happy to include him in their conversations, something that almost never happened at home.

"Between six and a half and seven," said Luca. "Knowing that allows you to get the proportions right."

"Don't you get them right just by looking at your models?" asked the boy.

"How many angels have *you* seen?" Luca shot back. "How many Virgin Marys? And let us say you wanted to create a truly heroic figure. Let us suppose, for example, that the only way Ludovico will pay Leonardo what he owes him is if Leonardo creates an heroic statue of *il Moro* to display in front of his castle. Well, just between you and me, Ludovico Sforza appears somewhat less than heroic in life—he is squat and portly—but if Leonardo wants to get paid, he will make that statue eight or even nine heads high, with long powerful legs that can gobble up the distance when marching or wrap themselves around a huge steed. There is no question that *il Moro* enjoys eating. By lengthening the body to eight heads, it will make him appear not only taller but less portly." He smiled. "And it's all mathematics."

"More to the point," put in Leonardo, "once I learn that a certain shape is pleasing to the eye, or that certain angles seem more appropriate than others, I need only codify the shape or the proportions or the angle in my notebooks and then it is there for me to use again whenever I wish. With mathematics I know how shadows fall at each moment of the day. Or let us say I wish to paint the assassination of Caesar. There will be many senators present, but they will not all be standing right next to him. They will be spread out all over the Senate floor, and with mathematics of perspective I can determine how small to make each of them in proportion to Caesar and Brutus."

"I see," said Mario, fascinated. "I had no idea math was so essential to art."

"It is self-evident," said Luca. "One simply cannot create an acceptable painting or sculpture without it."

I had better not mention the impressionists, or nonrepresentational art, thought Mario, resisting the urge to smile. *You would just get annoyed and tell me I'm wrong; and later Leonardo would question me endlessly about it, when he should be spending every spare minute finishing the painting before Sforza returns.*

Their food arrived—a roasted bird that Mario suspected wasn't a chicken—and while they ate Luca expounded upon his latest astronomical theories. Leonardo asked an occasional question and made an occasional comment, but it was clear that in this area, at least, Luca Pacioli was the master and Leonardo the pupil.

Leonardo, Bernardo, Luca, thought Mario, *they treat me like an equal, and they are three of the most interesting men I've ever met. The food's not bad, and I'm even getting used to the smells. I could even stay here an extra week or two, maybe a month, and really see the area, perhaps visit Florence or even to Rome.* A rat scuttled across the floor. Mario watched it without much interest. *It's amazing what faults you'll put up with when you weigh them against the virtues of a place. Or a time.*

After the table was cleared, a bowl of fruit was brought out. Neither Leonardo nor Luca wanted any; and as they got up to leave Mario, picked up a cluster of grapes to take home with him, When he saw Luca watching him, he smiled and said, "For later."

Which is true, he thought. *I didn't say who—or what—would be eating them later.*

Magic

"I don't believe it," said Leonardo, sitting on his favorite chair, absently stroking Melody's blue fur.

"It's true," replied Mario.

"But how is it possible?"

"I'm no doctor," said the boy. "I don't know *how* it's done, only that it is done."

"But how can you replace a heart without the patient dying? And how can you give him a dead man's heart, a heart that is no longer beating?"

"It's been commonplace for five hundred years," said Mario. "They have machines that can keep the donor's heart beating until they attach it to the host body."

"But surely the patient must die when they remove the damaged heart!" protested Leonardo. "No one can live without a heart, even in the twenty-sixth century!"

"The function of the heart is to pump blood. There are some major blood vessels leading out from the heart and others leading back in," explained Mario. "That's basic. We learned that in school.

What they do during a transplant is attach the blood vessels to a machine—a mechanical heart—that pumps the patient's blood while the exchange of hearts is made. Then they reattach the vessels to the new heart."

"But the agony alone will kill the patient. No man could stand the pain of having his chest cut open and his heart removed."

"There is no agony."

"Now I know that you are lying to me," said the artist accusingly.

"Have you any drugs in this era—substances that dull or alter the senses?"

"You mean like drinking strong spirits?" asked Leonardo.

"In a way. But I am talking about substances that, when properly administered, will put you to sleep and make you temporarily immune to pain."

"They actually have such substances?"

"For centuries."

"Magic!" murmured Leonardo.

"Science," replied Mario. "But science so far beyond what will be known during your lifetime that I'm sure it must seem like magic."

"Do they also transplant brains?" asked Leonardo. "Can one man's spirit live forever, moving from body to body?"

"No, they can't transplant brains—at least not yet. But they can grow new organs."

"You mean you can raise a young boy or girl and take his or her heart when you require it?" said Leonardo. "It sounds monstrous!"

"No," said Mario. "That would be murder."

"Then I don't understand."

"Hundreds of years from now they will discover a substance called DNA. There is a long scientific name for it that I have trouble pronouncing and that would mean nothing to you; but basically DNA is a genetic code, and it is different for every living thing."

"A genetic code?" repeated Leonardo, frowning. "You will have to explain that."

"DNA is a means of differentiating and identifying every human and animal that has ever lived. You will have to trust me on this, because I would have to use terms and concepts that are completely unknown to you to explain it in more detail." He paused, ordering his thoughts. "Each of us begins as a tiny entity, smaller than the tip of a pin. From that beginning we grow inside our mothers until it is time to be born, and we continue to grow to maturity. Now here is the tricky part: Every bit of us, even a single strand of hair, even the tiniest piece of skin, even our saliva, is filled with this identifying DNA that I mentioned. And the DNA remembers every aspect of ourselves, not just the hair or skin or saliva it came from. In the twenty-first century scientists were able to create duplicate organs from anyone by a process called cloning. Are you with me so far?"

"I am trying to comprehend," said Leonardo, frowning. "But it is very difficult."

"I know it must be," said Mario. "And probably an expert in cloning could explain it better, but I'm all you've got. Anyway, scientists found a way to tell this DNA, this code that exists in every tiny piece of you, how to reproduce your heart, lungs, liver, spleen—every part of you."

"To reproduce it?" said Leonardo, his face reflecting his confusion. "Without a sexual partner?"

"Without a sexual partner, and indeed without any effort on your part. The day you were born the hospital would collect a sample of your umbilical cord blood and freeze it against the day you required replacements. Then they would clone whatever you needed; and when the organs were ready, they would replace your sick or failing organs with new ones that were in every way identical, except for being healthy."

"Freeze my blood? You mean with ice? But ice melts. Suppose I needed this transplant in the summer?"

"Not with ice but with a machine that can generate freezing temperatures whatever the season."

"Magic!" muttered the artist again.

"Commonplace," said the boy.

"You can transplant hearts and create organs from hair and saliva," said Leonardo. "You can protect yourselves against every known disease. You can create mechanical hearts and can make yourselves immune to pain. What else is there?"

"There's so much I hardly know where to begin," said Mario. "You know that we have reached the stars, because you know Melody comes from the Antares system. But most of the planets we have discovered are inhospitable to humans, and because of that we have been unable to colonize them."

"So you cannot even set foot on them."

"Yes, we can," said Mario. "We've established outposts on water worlds, and ice worlds, and even airless worlds. What we haven't been able to do is populate them."

"How can you breathe on a world that has no air?"

"I saw your drawing of men walking along the ocean's floor. They have access to air." *Impractical access*, he added mentally, *but I won't tell you that unless you ask*. "The people of my era have access to air and to physical protection from the elements, even from heavier gravity."

"What do you mean, heavier gravity?" asked Leonardo.

"Not all worlds exert the same gravitational force on you," began the boy.

"Force? What force?"

"Let me put it another way," said Mario. "For reasons I can't explain to you, you won't weigh the same on every world. On some worlds it would be as if you were lighter than a feather and could leap to great heights, and on others it would seem as if you were carrying a hundred-pound rock on your back, which of course would limit what you would be able to do there. We have special clothing that will counteract such things, just as it will counteract poison in the air or no air at all." Mario stared at Leonardo, who was clearly groping with all these new concepts. "The problem," he continued, "is that these devices are very expensive to make and to transport, and limited in their use. So medical science is trying—"

"—to create a man who can breathe poison or no air at all!" interrupted Leonardo excitedly.

"That's right."

"If the world is entirely water, then he must have gills like a fish. If it has this heavy gravity you speak of, then he must be given limbs like an elephant to support his extra weight."

"That's what they're working on."

"They are usurping God's function."

"You don't approve?"

"No thinking man can disapprove of the pursuit of knowledge, only some of the uses to which it is put."

"That's an evasion."

"It depends on what you do on these worlds," answered Leonardo. "I disapprove of cutting open a man and removing his heart while he still lives. Any reasonable man would. But I do not object to cutting open that same man if he is immune to pain and replacing an unhealthy heart with a healthy one. So until I know exactly what you plan to do on each world, I can no more sit in judgment of you than a primitive savage can sit in judgment of me."

"Good answer," acknowledged Mario.

"Thank you," said Leonardo. "And now I have a question to ask you."

"Go ahead."

"Do men still die in the twenty-sixth century?"

"Yes, of course they do."

"I don't mean from accidents, or duels, or war."

"I know what you mean."

Leonardo frowned. "But if you have cured all disease and illness."

"We haven't," answered Mario. "New ones keep mutating and evolving."

"I do not understand those terms."

"Just believe me: There are always new diseases. As fast as we eliminate one forever, a new one comes along."

"But, barring disease, surely you stay young and beautiful forever."

"We stay young and healthy a lot longer," said Mario. "There are all kinds of cosmetic and medical treatments that can slow down the aging process, but eventually we all grow old and die."

"If your world is as crowded as you say, that is probably not a bad thing," said Leonardo.

"Nobody *wants* to grow old and feeble. We just want it to happen to the other guy."

"Still, it must be wonderful to be a doctor in your century," said the artist, "to know everything that is known about curing all the ills of the body."

Mario smiled. "It doesn't work that way."

"Explain, please."

"We know so much about each aspect of the body that a library of two thousand thick volumes couldn't contain all our knowledge. So—"

"So you live in an era when each doctor learns everything there is to know about one tiny aspect of the body," concluded Leonardo. "A doctor who can restore your vision cannot treat a broken leg." He paused. "It is very much like the magicians of myth. This one can cast spells, that one can battle dragons, this other one can fly."

Mario nodded. "You mentioned a broken leg. We have doctors who know everything there is to know about the knee but know *only* the knee, doctors who only know the ankle, doctors who only know the hips, doctors who only know the veins and arteries of the leg, doctors who only know the nerves in the leg, doctors who only rehabilitate injured legs."

"And of course they all know the secret of making you immune to pain."

The boy smiled. "No, almost none of them do. That is another area of specialization."

"At least there is work for everyone."

"Not with twenty-eight billion people on the planet," said Mario.

"That is a number for my friend Luca to conjure with," answered Leonardo. "It is far too many people for me to even imagine."

There was a knock at the door, and the artist walked over and opened it. A young man stood balanced on crutches, his left leg missing below the knee.

"This is for you," he said, handing a rolled paper to the artist.

"Thank you," said Leonardo.

The young man bowed awkwardly, then turned and began slowly making his way down the street.

Leonardo opened the paper and read it quickly.

"Another corpse," he announced. "A foolish young boy who fell from a tower. The body is so badly crushed that there will be nothing to learn from it, so I shall decline their invitation."

"Good," said Mario earnestly. "One dissection a day is about all I can handle."

"Did you see the young man who delivered the message?" asked the artist.

"Yes.

"Could your science grow him a new leg?"

"I don't know," said the boy. "But they could certainly give him an artificial leg that would look like the original and work even better."

"Magic!" said Leonardo admiringly.

Lefty

Leonardo was still displeased with the color of Cecilia's cheeks and began mixing his paints again, trying to come up with the exact shade he wanted.

"I'll never finish it in time," he said. "At this rate I might not even get her skin tones done in time." He sighed. "I hope there is enough light in my dungeon for me to read."

"You'll finish it," said Mario. "You just need to keep working at it."

"Painting is not that simple," insisted Leonardo, his frustration reflected in his voice.

"There are painters in the coming centuries, great painters, who have no difficulty turning out thirty or forty paintings in a year," noted the boy.

"I know, I know," growled Leonardo. "There are painters in Milan right now who can produce a painting a week. I won't speak of their quality."

"How old are you, Leonardo?" asked Mario.

"Thirty-eight," replied the artist.

"And how many paintings have you finished?"

"That is an unfair question."

"What's unfair about it?" asked the boy.

"It presupposes that I do nothing but paint, that I have no other interests in my life, that I am like your future artist whose Spanish-sounding name now eludes me." He paused to clear his throat, then continued. "But I am not just a painter. I am a scientist, and an architect, and an inventor, and a musician, and a sculptor. Not only that, but I am probably the greatest mountain climber on the entire peninsula." He stared at the boy. "I cannot and will not indulge one of my interests to the exclusion of the others."

"You didn't answer my question," said Mario.

"That's the best answer you're going to get," replied the artist gruffly.

"Have you averaged even one a year?"

"I don't have to put up with this!" snapped Leonardo irritably.

"No, you don't," agreed Mario. "You can simply wait for Ludovico Sforza to return home and then tell him you didn't finish the painting."

Suddenly the irritation and energy seemed to evaporate from Leonardo, and he slouched in defeat.

"I am sorry for losing my temper," he said in a gentler voice. "You are quite right. It is my own fault. I know I must finish the painting before *il Moro* comes back to Milan, and yet, even as I dabble with my palate, all I can think about are the medical wonders you related to me."

"It was my fault for distracting you," replied Mario. "The painting survives you by centuries, so I know that *someone* finished it. I just want it to be finished by you, and to turn out the way you want it to be."

"Whatever else I do, I will replace that cat with Melody," said Leonardo. "I must have a permanent record of the way she looks before you take her away."

"You have it in one of your notebooks. I saw all the drawings you made."

"But they are in black and white, while the painting will show her true color." Leonardo paused. "And the answer to your question is five."

"My question?" repeated Mario, puzzled.

"I have completed five paintings," admitted Leonardo.

"Plus some that you worked on during your apprenticeship. A few still survive, and people use them to study your development as an artist."

"And they know which parts I painted?"

"Yes," said Mario. "The parts you worked on are very distinctive."

"I wasn't that good then," said Leonardo. "I was still learning my craft, perfecting my techniques. I don't think my portions of the paintings stood out from the others."

"You underestimate the talent you displayed as a young man," said Mario. "And then there are the brushstrokes."

"Of course—the brushstrokes!" exclaimed Leonardo. "They don't call me *Mancino* for nothing."

"*Mancino?*"

"Does not the word still exist in your era?"

"I guess not," said the boy. "What does it mean?"

Leonardo grinned. "It means 'Lefty.' That's what Bernardo is always calling me. It is normal for me to paint with my left hand, so I forgot that the observer can tell that the brush strokes are exactly opposite to those of most painters."

"Centuries from now, when the authenticity of some of your paintings is in doubt, the presence or absence of those left-handed brushstrokes will help critics determine whether or not you were the actual artist."

"Thank you for telling me that," said Leonardo. "I have yet to have a left-handed student apply to be my apprentice, but now I know for certain that I shall not accept one. I would never want to be credited with an apprentice's clumsy work, and I would never want a left-handed apprentice to be credited with my better endeavors."

"You told me about writing from right to left," said the boy. "Do you find that being left-handed causes you to approach your painting differently as well?"

"I've never given it much thought," said Leonardo. "Let me see. Yes, now that you mention it, I do paint differently."

"In what way?"

"Except where I'm doing fine work, such as facial features, I find that I begin most of my brushstrokes at the lower right-hand end of the arc and curve upward to the left." He peered at the visible strokes on Cecilia's dress. "And most of the strokes are at their thickest where I begin, at the right." He straightened up. "Thank you, my young friend. I never noticed that before." Suddenly he walked over to the table that held his notebooks and began paging through them. "Yes, it's here in my sketches as well: lower right to upper left, thickest at the right, thinnest at the left." He put the books back down. "How very interesting to realize that it is a part of my technique to which I never really paid attention until this moment."

I would love to joke and say something like, well, you know what they say about left-handers, thought Mario. *But of course you have absolutely no idea what they say. Who besides Bernardo would dare tease the great Leonardo?*

Leonardo was still dwelling on his left-handedness. "Of course I start at the lower right," he said, more to himself than to Mario. "It is the same reason I taught myself to write from right to left. This way I don't drag the side of my hand across what I've just painted, and I can take longer strokes if needed."

"And Bernardo really calls you Lefty?"

"So does Luca, from time to time," replied Leonardo. "To them it's a term of endearment."

"Tell me," said Mario, "in your society is there any stigma attached to being left-handed?"

"None, though very few favor their left hands," answered the artist. "Why? Is there a stigma where you come from?"

"No," said the boy. "But there will come a time, still in your future but well in my past, when left-handedness will be considered a fault. Children will be taught to use their right hands, and some will actually be punished for favoring their left. Most early machines will be created for right-handed users. Then one day everyone seemed to have decided that being left-handed was acceptable, and there's never been any problem with it since then."

"If they had punished me for following my natural instinct, I would never have become a painter," said Leonardo. "I'd probably have spent more time studying mathematics with Luca and would even now be publishing the theory he wants to see—the one that proves that the Earth isn't the center of the universe."

"You have more important things to do," said Mario. "And besides, someone's already working on that theory."

"Oh?" said Leonardo quickly. "Who?"

I put my foot in it again, thought Mario unhappily. *If I stay here much longer, sooner or later I'm going to say something that will change history. I'll take Melody home and find that the race annihilated itself in the twentieth century, or that we're being ruled by chlorine-breathing aliens from Andromeda, or that we evolved into creatures with one eye and three legs—all because I told Leonardo something he wasn't supposed to know and he acted upon it; and a million permutations, none of which were supposed to exist, followed.*

"No one you know," said Mario at last. *Besides,* he added mentally, *I think Copernicus is still a teenager.*

Leonardo went back to mixing his colors, still dissatisfied with the hues he was producing.

"I've been thinking about the substance you mentioned that's in every portion of us," said the artist.

"DNA?"

Leonardo nodded. "That's it. I wonder what this code looks like?"

It looks like a double helix, which I can't tell you, thought the boy. Aloud he said, "I think it takes many pages of very small print to write out a single sample of it."

"Then it's for Luca, not for me."

"Speaking of codes, there was a time, centuries in my past, when you were thought to have hidden one in your work."

"A code?" repeated Leonardo.

"That's right."

"A code to what?"

"Believe it or not, the Holy Grail."

"If I knew where the Grail was, I wouldn't leave codes for others," snorted Leonardo. "I'd go find it and claim it for myself."

"So you believe the Grail was a cup?"

"A cup, a chalice, a goblet," said Leonardo. "Why? What do *you* think it was?"

"The same," replied the boy. "Do you belong to any secret societies?"

Leonardo looked genuinely amused. "You've spent some time with me. When do you think I'd have as much as a spare minute for a secret society?"

"Just wondering."

"Just answering," said the artist.

Leonardo continued mixing his paints for a few minutes and finally uttered an annoyed curse.

"I am simply not getting the color I want," he announced. "Let us go for a walk. It will help to clear my head, and then I can go back to work with fresh eyes." He looked at Melody, who was sleeping peacefully at his feet. "And tonight I will begin putting you in Prospero's place. If a blue pet from the stars doesn't make this painting memorable, I don't know what will."

Philosophers

"Magnificent, is it not?" said Leonardo, standing with his hands on his hips and staring at the huge cathedral.

"It hasn't changed from your era to mine," said Mario. "There must be forty spires. In a way it reminds me of Cairo."

"You have been to Cairo?"

The boy nodded. "Yes. It was once called the City of Ten Thousand Minarets. Many of them have decayed, but it still has a few hundred remaining."

"But those are the mosques of Islam, and this is the Cathedral of Milan," said the artist.

"They're both awesome sights, and they're monuments to God. That makes them similar in a way."

Leonardo smiled. "Well said, my young friend. The churches and mosques are like the bodies I paint and sculpt—they are the outer garments of the soul."

A small, wiry man began walking toward them.

"Is that Luca Pacioli?" asked Mario, peering at him.

"No," replied the artist. "We won't find Luca at a cathedral, except perhaps to climb to the very top of it so he can better observe the stars." He paused. "It is best that I don't encounter him again until after you have returned to your home in the future."

"Why? I thought he was your friend."

"He is," said Leonardo. "But he is also the smartest man I know. Sooner or later he would figure out that you are not what we have said you were—and if he should ever see Melody . . ."

"You have a point," said Mario. "Maybe we should return to your house right now, before we run into him."

"I took you to the Cathedral precisely because this is the one place I knew we wouldn't meet him," said Leonardo. He turned to the boy. "Tell me about the church of your era."

"It's still standing."

"I don't mean the Cathedral of Milan," said the artist. "I mean the Christian religion."

"*It*'s still standing too," said Mario.

"But there have been so many changes," said Leonardo. "What do the priests say about taking one man's heart and putting it in another man's chest?"

"They don't do that anymore," said the boy. "Maybe I wasn't clear about that when we discussed it. They did it in the twentieth and twenty-first centuries—that, and they also use self-contained mechanical hearts. But by the twenty-second century, we were cloning our own organs, and the only things transferred to our bodies were our own replacement organs, created from our own DNA."

"It occurs to me that if you have visited other worlds, perhaps you have encountered men, or at least thinking creatures, living there."

"Living creatures like Melody, yes. Thinking creatures, not yet—but I suppose it's only a matter of time."

"I feel very sorry for the priests of your era," said Leonardo.

"Why?"

"How will they convince a thinking creature they find living on another world that Christ died for its sins?"

The boy looked surprised. "I've never considered it. If there are aliens who don't worship God, why should they believe beings from another world?" He seemed lost in thought for a moment. "What if they have their own religion and try to convince us that we are wrong, that Jesus was just a man. What if they can *prove* their religion is the true one?"

"Since any religion that denies Jesus cannot be the true religion, God will show us how to answer their arguments, as he shows us how to answer such arguments here on Earth," said Leonardo calmly.

"But if—"

"It was just an idle speculation," said Leonardo. "It is nothing that you or I have to worry about. Would you like to see the inside of the Cathedral?"

"I've seen it," said Mario. When Leonardo looked surprised, he added, "A thousand years from now."

"By then it will doubtless be filled with devices I would find incomprehensible," suggested the artist.

"One or two," acknowledged Mario. "But for the most part, people seem to like their religion and their churches to remain traditional."

"Do they still paint the Crucifixion and the Ascension?"

"Yes," answered the boy. "Not as often perhaps, but yes, they still do."

"I find that comforting," said Leonardo. "It is good to know that some things will continue to exist."

"I do not mean to imply that the entire world is Christian," said Mario.

"I know," said the artist. "You already mentioned that Islam still exists."

"So do Judaism, and Buddhism, and Hinduism, and many other religions as well."

"Are the different religions getting along better in the future?" asked Leonardo.

The boy shrugged. "It depends on the year and the country—and probably the time of day and which way the wind is blowing."

"That is a shame," said the artist. "I simply assumed that men will have learned to live in harmony in another thousand years."

"Oh, they don't go to war over religion anymore," said Mario. "The weapons of my era are too deadly and too efficient. I just meant that people of different faiths tend to live and marry within their own culture and religion."

"They always have."

"Probably," agreed the boy. "But I think things may be changing soon."

"Oh? In what way?"

"We know that there is life on other worlds," said Mario. "Eventually we'll find intelligent life. It'll probably be so different from us that we'll realize how very trivial our differences are. Muslim, Jew,

Christian—we all worship the same God. That gives us a lot more in common with one another than with intelligent creatures that breathe chlorine, eat poison, and smell colors."

Leonardo looking at him admiringly. "Your parents must be very proud of you."

"My parents would be anything but proud if they knew I let Melody run off in Renaissance Milan," said Mario. The muscles in his jaw tightened. "I miss them."

"That is only natural."

"And even though I will return to my era only seconds after I left," continued the boy, "I can't help feeling that somehow they know I'm gone and are worrying about me. I'm all they've got."

"Don't you have any siblings?"

Mario shook his head. "The Earth is already too crowded. Most families are encouraged to have only one child."

Leonardo smiled. "And after the Black Death, we were encouraged to go forth and multiply so that we could repopulate Europe."

"I guess that is one thing that hasn't changed," said Mario ruefully. "The government still involves itself in our daily lives."

"That is the nature of government."

"I thought it was to protect us from enemies and provide certain civic services," said the boy.

"That is the *purpose* of government," said Leonardo. "But the *nature* of government is to meddle whenever and wherever possible. And as you confirm, it hasn't changed."

"You are blocking my way," said an annoyed voice from behind them.

They turned to find themselves facing a tall, burly peddler pushing a wooden cart, and atop the cart were a number of birds in wooden cages.

"Oh, it's you, Leonardo," said the peddler. "You were facing the Cathedral, and I didn't recognize you from behind."

"If you continue to lie to me, Francesco, you will lose my business," said Leonardo, looking mildly amused.

"All right," said Francesco the peddler. "I spotted you and thought you might want to do our usual business."

Leonardo looked at the various birds and finally pointed to a small yellow one. "This one," he said.

"Just one today?" asked Francesco.

"Just one."

"Sforza hasn't paid you yet, eh?" said the peddler.

"Does everyone in this city know my finances?" said Leonardo wearily.

"Oh, there's probably three or four who don't," replied Francesco with a grin. "I'll make you a bargain, Leonardo."

"Let me hear it," said the artist, eyeing him suspiciously.

"I'll trade you a bird for a bird. Draw one on the side of my cart and you can have another."

"Done!" said Leonardo. He took a stick of charcoal out of his pocket and quickly sketched a bird on the cart, just above one of the wheels.

"Only one head and two wings," said Francesco, looking quite amused with himself. "I won't pay double for a two-headed bird."

"Maybe I'll just remove his head and feet and draw him as he appears on your dinner table," said Leonardo without looking up.

"Draw me as well, and I'll toss in another bird."

"The world is not ready for a true representation of you," said Leonardo sardonically. "It would cause women to faint and give small children nightmares."

"He's afraid to draw me," said Francesco to Mario, "because he knows if he does, every subject will want to look just like me." He laughed at his own joke.

"Finished," said Leonardo, straightening up and stepping aside so Francesco could see the drawing.

"Now I can prove to everyone that the great Leonardo buys his birds from Francesco!" said the peddler happily.

Leonardo handed him a coin. "This is for the yellow one, and the drawing is for another." He studied the cages again. "The white one, I think."

"Whatever you say."

Francesco opened the door to the white bird's cage, reached in, grabbed the bird, pulled it out, and then released it. It promptly flew off, and he repeated the procedure with the yellow bird.

"I'll see you tomorrow, Leonardo," said the peddler, humming a happy tune as he pushed his cart down the street.

"Do you do this all the time—buy birds and set them free?" asked Mario.

"How can I learn the principles of flight if I do not see birds in flight?" replied the artist.

"You could take the birds home and let them fly around your studio, and then you would still have them to study again the next day," said Mario.

"Perhaps," said Leonardo. "But birds are not men. If you take away their freedom, they do not fight to regain it." He shrugged. "I think God meant them to be free to fly high in the sky. I am merely helping Him realize His goals." He looked at Mario. "Why do you stare at me with such a strange expression?"

"Because I am proud to know such an enlightened man in a not-very-enlightened era," said Mario.

"Thank you."

"It makes me think," continued the boy. "If I were to stay here in this era, maybe I could help bring enlightenment."

Leonardo shook his head. "You're place is with your parents, and you will be returning there in a few more days."

"Maybe it isn't," said the boy. "Maybe I'm supposed to stay here. Maybe I even helped bring about the Renaissance."

"If you did, there would be a record of it, and you would know it," said Leonardo reasonably. "You know about me, and about other artists of this age. Why do you not know that a boy named Mario came from the future and changed the way everyone thought?"

"Maybe I used a different name."

"Do you really believe that is what happened, or will happen?"

"There is so much opportunity here!" said the boy. "I could make a difference! I have heard more interesting conversations and seen more interesting things this week than in my whole life!"

"Do you not see, then, that it is your era you must live in and change, not mine?" asked Leonardo gently.

And because he was honest with himself, Mario realized unhappily that the artist was right.

Lady with a Cat

They returned to Leonardo's house, and the artist spent the next half hour simply staring at the painting of Cecilia, a deepening frown on his handsome features.

"What's the problem?" asked Mario.

"The proportions will be wrong," said Leonardo at last. "Melody is simply not a cat, her structure is different, and Cecilia's arms and hands are positioned to hold Prospero. The painting will be out of balance."

I mustn't speak, thought Mario. *It doesn't matter that I know you didn't paint the cat. You've got to decide it on your own.*

Finally Leonardo sighed deeply. "I suppose if I can change the painting to eliminate the window and alter the background, I can change the position of her hands and arms." He extended his left forefinger and traced the changes he wanted to make in the air. "Yes, it will work. But it will take still more time, and *il Moro* won't stay away forever."

"When I first arrived here, you told me your apprentices are due back in two weeks," Mario reminded him. "Perhaps they can work on it."

"The sky, the solid colors, these they can do under my supervision," agreed the artist. "But the fine work—Cecilia's facial features, her hands, Melody, the positioning of their bodies—these I must do myself if it is to be a painting by Leonardo."

He stood back and stared at the portrait.

"I hate that cat," he said, "but I must admit I did well by him."

"There's not much of him left," noted Mario. "You got rid of him—well, most of him—the other night."

"I can still see his every detail, even to the smug expression on his feline face."

Mario peered at the painting. "Where?"

Leonardo smiled and tapped his temple with the same forefinger he had been waving. "In here."

"Do you see a painting in your imagination before you sit down to work on it?" asked the boy.

"It depends on the painting," answered Leonardo. "If, for example, it is a painting of Jesus or the Virgin or the saints, then yes, I position all the characters in my mind until I am pleased with the form. Then I begin sketching each character, every aspect of the painting, before I actually begin applying paint to a walnut slab."

"Do you do all your painting on walnut?"

"No, I am constantly experimenting with surfaces and textures as well as with paints. But to answer the rest of your question, when I am painting a living model, such as Cecilia, I position her exactly the way I want her, and then I begin sketching and painting."

"Do you paint things you've never seen?"

"You know I have painted the Messiah and the saints," replied the artist.

"But they were men—or at least Jesus appeared in human form during his time on Earth. I was thinking of angels and demons."

"I can paint anything I can imagine," answered Leonardo. "Any competent artist can. But there must be a reason to paint it, a purpose behind it. To date, I have had no reason to paint demons and devils, nor have I painted any of the creatures of mythology—the centaur, the cyclops, the minotaur, the sirens, creatures like that."

"Why not?"

"I am a realist and a scientist," replied Leonardo. "There are enough things in this world that I do not yet understand that I do not have to add creatures of the imagination." He stared at the portrait. "What possible purpose would be served by giving Cecilia wings? I would rather give her an expression, a pseudo life, that will move those who view the painting. I was in the process of doing the same thing for Prospero, much as I detested him."

"You don't seem like an animal hater to me," said Mario. "What was it about that particular cat that annoyed you so greatly?"

"He wouldn't hold still," said Leonardo.

"That's *it*?" said Mario, surprised. "That's the only reason?"

"I am not a fast worker." Suddenly Leonardo smiled. "Most people would say that was an understatement," he said with an amused chuckle. "Anyway, every time the cat changed position, it also changed the way Cecilia held her arms, or positioned her fingers."

"But surely you first sketched what you wanted," said the boy.

"You knew how she would hold her arms and fingers, how the material of her dress would lay, so why couldn't you simply use your sketchbook rather than your models?"

Leonardo walked over to the sketchbook in question and opened it. There were pages upon pages of drawings of Prospero, still more of Cecilia, some consisting of nothing but her hands or the cat's head.

"Do you see any shadings of color here?" asked Leonardo. "Do you see the glow in her cheeks, the light in her eye as the sun catches it?"

"No, of course not," said Mario. "They're just sketches, black on white."

"That's right," said the artist. "And the next time I'm commissioned to do a painting using only black and white, maybe I will be able to rely entirely on my sketchbook; but until then, I prefer live models."

"How do you paint Jesus?"

"I use a model, and then I paint the face that I see in my mind. But I need a model for the colors and shadings. Or, let me say, I much prefer a model."

"A thought just occurred to me," said Mario.

"Oh?"

"What will Cecilia say when she sees the painting and her cat isn't in it?"

"In all immodesty, the rest of the painting does her such justice that she'll get over her disappointment in a matter of minutes."

"You make her sound very shallow," said the boy.

Leonardo shook his head. "Not shallow. Just young. I think eventually *il Moro* will arrange a marriage for her to one of the nobles in his court so he can continue to see her. And she will continue to cultivate her interest in art, literature, and music." He considered the portrait, then nodded his head. "Yes, she will become quite an admirable and intelligent woman. She is simply young, not shallow."

"I am young too," said Mario.

"Yes," agreed Leonardo, "but you know so many of the secrets of the Universe, how could you possibly be shallow, my young friend?"

"All I know is that certain things will work in my era," said Mario. "I don't know how they will work."

"For a boy your age, that is enough," said the artist. "You have seen the future. *How* I envy you!"

"But you have helped *create* the future. Millions of men over the eons will envy you."

"They would envy me less if they had to pay my bills or deal with my patron," said Leonardo sardonically. He sighed deeply. "And my future with *il Moro* could be of limited duration if I do not get back to work on the painting."

"I didn't mean to distract you."

"It's all right." Leonardo flashed him a guilty smile. "*Everything* distracts me. That is why I have left a trail of so many unfinished paintings and projects in my wake."

Suddenly he walked to the kitchen and came back a moment later with a pewter goblet filled with wine. He stood before the portrait and raised the goblet aloft.

"*Lady with a Cat,*" he intoned, "I have lived with you for more than a year. Tonight I bid you farewell, for before I retire for the evening, every last trace of the detested Prospero will be gone."

And so saying, he bowed to the portrait and drained his goblet.

NINETEEN

Lady with an Alien

"What can her world be like, to have legs jointed in such strange places?" asked Leonardo as he studied Melody's physical structure.

"I've never been there," replied Mario. "I've never been to any other world," he added unhappily. "But I know it's an oxygen world or she couldn't breathe our air, and it has to have a similar gravity."

"Why similar?"

"If it were lighter than Earth," said the boy, "she would run out of strength and energy very quickly. Just the act of walking, using muscles that were made for lighter gravity, would soon tire her out; and that has never happened. And the gravity isn't heavier, because her strength doesn't seem out of proportion to her size."

Leonardo frowned. "Explain, please."

"If her world had twice Earth's gravity," replied Mario, "the muscles she developed to get around there would be so powerful that she could leap three or four meters into the air on Earth, and I've never seen her do that. Once in a while when I hold her, she wriggles to get free, and I have no problem keeping my grip on her; I wouldn't be able to do so if her world had a much heavier gravity."

"I see," said Leonardo. "I suppose when you get right down to it, it's no stranger for her legs to be jointed like that than for an elephant to have four knees, or a spider eight legs, or a snake no legs at all."

"Or for a bird to fly, or a fish to breathe water," put in Mario.

"God is endlessly inventive," said Leonardo. He sighed wistfully. "Still, it would be wonderful to see the things she has seen, to set foot on another world, to see creatures no one has seen before or even imagined, to look up into the sky and see a different configuration of stars." He grimaced. "To not be surrounded by so-called scholars and astronomers who swear the Earth is the center of the universe. Yes, little Melody—I envy you."

Melody, who had been sleeping on a table next to some notebooks, stood up, stretched herself fore and aft, and then leaped gently into Mario's arms. The boy caught her easily and began stroking her fur.

"As long as you're holding her, sit on the chair," said Leonardo. Mario was about to sit down next to the table, but Leonardo waved him away. "No, the one over there, where Cecilia sits when I paint her. Now turn and look off to your left. No, don't turn your whole body, just your head, and perhaps swing your left shoulder just a bit. Here, let me position you."

Leonardo walked over and posed the boy exactly as Cecilia had posed.

"Now Melody is facing in the wrong direction," said Leonardo. "No, don't you move. I'll take care of it." He took Melody from the boy, then returned her, facing the way he wanted.

The artist studied his two subjects. "Move your left arm just a bit, so I can more clearly see your fingers—and stretch them out." Leonardo stared intently at Melody. "She has a much longer body than Prospero. I am clearly going to have to re-paint the fourth and fifth fingers on Cecilia's hand. If I don't, it will look like Melody is slipping out of her grasp and onto the floor."

Melody, tiring of the attention, tried to twist free from Mario.

"Hold her!" instructed Leonardo. "Shades of Prospero! What is it about me that makes small animals want to wriggle and jump to the floor?" Then, suddenly, his face brightened. "I have an idea. Wait here. I'll be right back." He walked to the kitchen and returned with two grapes. He offered one to Melody, who immediately began eating it. When she finished, he let her see that he had another grape in his hand and then stood exactly where he wanted the little animal to look.

"That's it!" exclaimed the artist, studying her body and expression. "That's it exactly!" He grabbed a sketchbook and began drawing furiously while Mario tried to keep Melody from jumping down and running over to Leonardo to grab the second grape.

Finally Leonardo closed his sketchbook. "All right," he said. "You can let her go now."

The instant Mario released his grip the little animal raced across the floor and took the grape from the artist.

"It will work!" said Leonardo excitedly. "In fact, the proportions will work even better than with the cat! Tonight marks the birth of *Lady with an Alien*." He began pacing up and down excitedly. "As soon as I can match the blue of her fur, and use it in portions of the sky."

And suddenly he froze, motionless.

"What is it?" asked Mario. "Are you all right?"

Leonardo turned slowly to face the boy. "I can't do it, can I?" he said. "I can't paint *Lady with an Alien* if I am to keep your secret."

Mario stared at him but made no reply.

"How can I present *il Moro* with a painting of a blue animal that has never been seen before? Half of his court would think I was drunk, and the other half would think I was mad. And Sforza himself, whichever side he chose, would never agree to pay me for it, and an entire year's work would have gone for nothing." He looked accusingly at the boy. "You might have told me that before letting me get so excited."

"*Lady with an Alien* doesn't exist in my era," answered Mario, choosing his words carefully. "There is no record of it ever having existed, so I knew that you wouldn't paint it." *Now just don't ask me what you did paint, and maybe I won't have influenced the past—and perhaps the future as well.*

"I will not put that cat back into the painting," said Leonardo adamantly. "Let me think."

He began pacing again, slower and less excitedly this time, pausing every minute or two to look at either Melody or the painting.

"I think I have an idea," he finally announced.

"What is it?"

"Let me see if it works first," said Leonardo. He picked up his sketchbook and began making slight changes to the drawings he had made of Melody, then added a number of notes, scribbling them from right to left.

When he was finished, he picked up the book, opened it to the pages he'd been working on, and carried it over to Melody, who lay sprawled on a bookshelf at eye level. He stared intently at her, made a few more changes to his drawings, and finally tossed the sketchbook back onto the table.

"It will work," said Leonardo.

"What will?"

Leonardo smiled. "You shall see," he promised, as he began working on Cecilia's portrait. "In the meantime, say a brief prayer for the short-lived *Lady with an Alien.*"

TWENTY

Lady with an Ermine

Leonardo sketched furiously for almost an hour, oblivious to Mario's presence, indeed to anything except his notebook. Finally he put the notebook down on a table and looked at Melody, who was once again sprawled on a bookshelf.

"Sweet little Melody," he said. "I have decided to give you a change of clothing."

"What are you talking about?" asked Mario.

"I am talking about putting Melody in my painting of Cecilia," answered the artist.

"But you already explained why you can't do that," said Mario uneasily. *My God,* he thought, *what if I can't talk him out of it, and he paints her, and when I go back the future is changed because of it, and my parents aren't my parents?*

Leonardo smiled. "Only you and I will know it is Melody, and I won't tell anyone if you don't."

"I don't understand."

"Look at this," said Leonardo, opening the notebook.

"It's Melody," said Mario. He frowned. "But it's not *quite* Melody. The legs look wrong, and you've made her coat look pale, though I suppose you'll color it in later. And her mouth looks a little different too."

"But there's no question in your mind that it's Melody?" persisted the artist.

"None."

Still smiling, Leonardo took a book down from the top shelf, thumbed through it until he found what he was looking for, and laid it open on the table. "And what do you think of this?" he asked.

Mario walked over and stared at the page. "It's not identical to your drawing, but it's similar."

"As similar to it as Melody is?"

Mario looked again, then nodded his head. "It's as close in one direction as Melody is in the other, if that makes sense to you."

"So when I show you the sketch I made, you reasonably conclude that it's Melody because she is your pet and you know her," said Leonardo.

"That's right."

"But if I were to show this sketch to someone who had never seen Melody, that person would think it is the animal in the book, am I correct?"

"I suppose so," said Mario.

"Then it is solved," said Leonardo. "That animal is an ermine, and the painting will become *Lady with an Ermine*."

Mario felt an enormous wave of relief sweep over him. *You got it right*, he thought. *With no hints or help from me, you came up with the right painting and the right title.*

"Furthermore, the ermine is the perfect animal for this particular painting," continued Leonardo.

"Oh? Why?"

"Two reasons," said Leonardo, looking inordinately pleased with himself. "Cecilia's last name is Gallerani, and the Greek word for 'ermine' is *galee*. She will be so flattered that I will hear very little about removing Prospero from the painting."

"I thought I read somewhere that you didn't know Greek," said Mario.

"I was not allowed to study Greek in school," answered the artist, "but that doesn't mean I could not study it on my own."

"All right," said Mario. "What is the other reason?"

"*Il Moro* himself received the insignia of the Order of the Ermine not two years ago."

"What is the Order of the Ermine?"

"A very prestigious society devoted to the ideal of chivalry," answered Leonardo. "It is a great honor to have been inducted into it. In fact, Sforza has been nicknamed *Italico Morel Bianco Ermellino*— Italian Moor, White Ermine. He is such an egotist that he will assume I chose the ermine to honor him; and as I said, Cecilia will assume I chose it to honor her name. Only you and I will know the real reason that I replaced Prospero with Melody." He smiled. "I think I have just purchased my freedom."

"I feel just like a conspirator," said Mario, returning Leonardo's smile.

"I'll tell you another reason he will be pleased with it," continued the artist. "The ermine has been a symbol of chastity for at least the past thousand years."

"I didn't know that," admitted Mario.

"But *il Moro* knows it," said Leonardo. "And since he is perhaps the least chaste man of my acquaintance, he will be cynically pleased that his foolish painter obviously thinks of him as the personification of purity."

"Won't he be more likely to think that it represents Cecilia's purity?" asked Mario.

Leonardo shook his head. "His thoughts rarely extend beyond himself—but *she* will think so, and that is another reason she will not object to Prospero being eliminated from the painting." He paused. "Yes, it is an elegant solution. I think it will solve all my problems."

"Not quite all," Mario pointed out. "Sforza's coming home in less than three weeks. You still have to finish it."

"But now that I know what I am going to do, I'll spend the next week painting this version of Melody that I have sketched, and then my apprentices can complete the painting under my direction. I have one in particular, a boy named Salai, about your age, who shows enormous promise. The others can paint the sky; he will be charged with any changes in Cecilia's arms and hands."

"My age?" repeated Mario. "I'm only sixteen. Isn't that young to be working as an apprentice?"

"What else is he to do?" asked Leonardo curiously.

"I will be going to school for another ten years, maybe longer."

"You have more to learn in your era than we do in ours," said Leonardo. "Ten more years. Why, you'll be halfway to the grave by the time your life is starting." He paused and sighed. "Besides, Salai is illegitimate. Most formal education is forbidden to him, as it was to me."

"Are all your apprentices illegitimate?"

Leonardo nodded. "They did not ask to be born. Someone must care for them."

"You are a good man," said Mario. "I am glad that we met."

"You say that as if you are about to leave," said Leonardo.

"I kept my end of the bargain," said Mario. "I went over your notebooks, I told you what I was allowed to tell you, as well as a few things I am probably not allowed to tell you. I wish I could stay longer, I wish I could spend years here—but it's time I returned home."

"I need three more days, possibly four," said Leonardo.

"What for?"

"What have we been talking about?" replied the artist. "I must turn Melody into an ermine." He looked sharply at Mario. "But you knew that all along, didn't you? You know that no painting called *Lady with a Cat* or *Lady with an Alien* ever existed, so of course you must have known that I would paint *Lady with an Ermine*."

Mario smiled once more, but offered no reply.

The Fingerprint

Three days had passed, and Leonardo had inserted Melody into the painting with all the considerable skill at his disposal. He was starting to make sketches of the new position of Cecilia's hands and fingers when Mario entered the studio.

"Thanks for letting me sleep," said the boy.

"You looked tired," replied the artist. "And besides, I had Melody to keep me company." He reached down and ran his fingers through the bright blue fur of the little animal, who wriggled happily at his touch.

"Were you painting all night long?"

"When I work, I work," answered Leonardo.

"It looks very nice," said Mario, indicating the painting.

"I am quite pleased with it," answered Leonardo. "In all immodesty, I consider it to be my best to date."

"I agree."

"In fact, I would be content to let my reputation as a painter rest upon *Lady with an Ermine*."

"Posterity won't agree with you," said Mario. "Which is just as well, since by the time they get through trying to preserve it by over-painting it, the authorship will be in doubt."

"You mean people of your era merely *think* I painted *Lady With an Ermine*—that no one knows for sure?"

"I didn't say that," replied the boy. "There is no doubt that you are the artist."

"Then I don't understand."

"There will be uncertainty for a few centuries, but eventually it will be proved beyond a doubt."

"By the same mysterious machine you told me about that uses those invisible lights?"

"An X-ray machine?" said Mario. "No, it will be much simpler than that."

"I do not sign my paintings," said Leonardo adamantly. "I will not make an exception for this one."

"Of course not," said Mario reasonably. "If you signed it, there would never be any doubt who painted it. Even if they painted over your name, the experts of my era would be able to uncover it."

"But you told me they couldn't determine the color of the sky," Leonardo pointed out.

"Colors are more difficult. But they can find any lines that have been painted over."

"But since I will not sign my name, how will they know?"

Mario sighed. "It requires me to tell you something you are not supposed to know." He lowered his head in thought, then looked up. "If I show you, if I help you arrange it so that someday far in the future it will be proven that you are the artist, will you give me your solemn promise never to use that knowledge or impart it to anyone else?"

"I promise," said Leonardo.

"All right," said Mario. "I want you to do something. Walk over to the painting and place your right thumb, very gently, on the rendering of Melody's neck."

"Why?"

"I'll explain in a moment. Just do as I ask—and remember, very lightly. Don't press against it."

Leonardo followed the boy's instructions, then stepped back. Mario approached the painting, leaned over until he was mere inches from it, and finally nodded his approval.

"That's the first step," he announced.

"There's more?"

"Not today, possibly not even this year," said Mario. "But the next time you paint a portrait, press your thumb lightly against some portion of it before the paint hardens."

"And then?"

"That's all."

"And this will identify me as the artist?" said Leonardo disbelievingly.

"Yes."

"Please explain."

"I will," said Mario. "And remember your promise." He walked over, took a hold of Leonardo's right hand, and held it up before the artist's face. "Do you see these tiny lines in your fingers?"

"Yes, of course. Everyone has them."

"That is true," said the boy. "But what you don't know is that no two are identical. We call them fingerprints, and before we discovered DNA—that coded material I told you about a few nights ago—fingerprints were the main form of identification. Starting about four centuries from now, almost every baby born in Europe will have its fingerprints taken and put on file at birth."

"But that is four hundred years from now," said Leonardo. "What has that to do with me?"

"I told you that no two people have identical fingerprints. No painting you do from this day on will ever be credited to anyone else. Just remember to put your print on the next one. Then, in the middle of the twentieth century, someone will discover your thumbprint on the ermine, match it against a print they know is yours from another painting, and then you will once again be credited as the artist of *Lady with an Ermine*."

"Fascinating!" The artist leaned forward and squinted at the fingerprint. "And that is Leonardo?"

"No," replied Mario. "That is just a means of identifying Leonardo, like your name or your signature—or your face, for that matter. These things are all on the surface. The real Leonardo, that which makes Leonardo unique from all others, exists beneath the surface, *here*"—he gently touched the artist's head—"and especially *here*." He touched Leonardo's heart.

"I think that you have grown far more than three weeks' wiser during the time you have been here," said Leonardo.

"Thank you," said Mario. "And remember your promise."

"I shall. I will also sleep easier, knowing that eventually my name and my painting will be reunited, thanks to you."

"You would have touched it anyway," said Mario. "After all, it's there a thousand years from now, and it was there before I came back looking for Melody."

"Let me pose you a riddle, my young friend," said Leonardo. "If it was there before you visited me, that means the painting existed before you visited me—but why is it a painting of Melody rather than Prospero?"

Mario was still pondering that paradox when he decided that it was time for him and Melody to return home.

Lady with a Smile

"And you say I will create a greater painting than this?" said Leonardo, staring at *Lady with an Ermine*.

"More than one," replied Mario. *Including a lady with an enigmatic smile that will fascinate everyone who sees it for the next thousand years.*

"Can you tell me anything about them?"

Mario shook his head. "I'm sorry."

"I understand," said Leonardo. "But it is very frustrating."

"For me too." The boy leaned down, picked up Melody, and tucked her under an arm. "I have very much enjoyed meeting you," he said, extending his hand.

"My friend Machiavelli recently told me that opportunities to change my life were few and far between," said Leonardo. "*You* have changed my life, and I thank you for it."

"As you have enriched mine," replied Mario.

"I will miss you," said Leonardo. He shook Mario's hand, then ran his fingers lightly over Melody's head. "I will miss you both."

Mario took one last look around the room, trying to fix it forever in his memory—the piles of notebooks, the painting on its walnut panel, the bookshelves, the wooden chairs, the pewter goblets, and Leonardo himself. Finally he walked to the door, and opened it.

Then, just before he left, he turned back to Leonardo.

"Do you know a woman named Lisa?" he asked.

"No," said the artist.

A smile spread across Mario's face.

"You will," he promised, just before he stepped out into the street. "You will."

Leonardo's Life and Art

The late twentieth and early twenty-first centuries became the Age of Specialization. If you were a doctor, you handled one particular aspect of the human body (or else you sent your patient to such a specialist); no brain surgeon ever operated on a knee. If you were a lawyer, you dealt in one single aspect of the law; no corporate lawyer ever faced a jury in a murder trial. If you were a professional golfer, you didn't participate in tennis tournaments.

Leonardo was a specialist, too—but unlike today's men and women, Leonardo specialized in everything. His wide range of interests and knowledge literally defines the ideal of the Renaissance man.

He left behind 20,000 pages of notes and sketches. That comes to about 700 books the size of this one. In them, we see the first enlightened mind of his era coping with the concept of flight, with the structure and musculature of the human body, with the anatomy of birds, with such diverse notions as tanks, bicycles, hydraulics systems, bridges, and architecture. Long before his death he probably knew more about each subject than any man alive.

He experimented as he painted. He was among the first to use oils. He perfected the use of red chalk. He created or perfected the various techniques mentioned in *Lady with an Alien*.

He had a beautiful singing voice. He could accompany himself on musical instruments he created. He was said to be a very handsome young man.

He was a skilled mountain climber.

And, oh yes, he could paint.

The *Mona Lisa* is unquestionably the most famous painting in the world. *The Last Supper*, though faded—Leonardo used an experimental technique that didn't work very well—certainly ranks among the top ten.

Yet his breakthrough painting was *Lady with an Ermine*. That was the first so-called modern painting ever done, and it clearly pleased Ludovico Sforza, who remained his patron until he was overthrown by the French.

Given Leonardo's fame, which extended throughout Italy and France during his lifetime and has never diminished, it is amazing that the ownership of the painting was unknown for two centuries after his death. It finally surfaced in Poland, where it remains to this day.

Many parts of *Lady with an Ermine* were overpainted when the original paint began flaking off, and for that reason the original painter's identity was in question until the middle of the last century. The technique and the clear presence of left-handed brush strokes on Cecilia's hands and on the ermine (which looks much more like a ferret in size and color) led most art scholars to conclude that Leonardo was the original painter. The clincher came when they discovered his barely visible thumbprint on the ermine.

For all his accomplishments, Leonardo must have driven some of his patrons crazy. The list of his unfinished projects—paintings, sculptures, bridges, war machines—is almost as long as his completed ones. The man's mind was so active, he was so interested in everything around him, he was so curious about the world in which he lived, that he seemed unable to concentrate on any one project for any length of time. (Example: There have been books and movies about how long it took Michelangelo to paint the ceiling of the Sistine Chapel, and yet he painted it—the entire thing—in less time than it took Leonardo to paint the *Mona Lisa*.)

Did Leonardo spend all that time, each day, every day, painting? Of course not. A thousand things captured his attention, a hundred potential projects piqued his interest. (That he finished the *Mona Lisa*—or any of his paintings—shows a certain unappreciated discipline, given the range of his interests.)

Leonardo was always short of money, possibly because he liked to live well, play host to many friends, feed and house many apprentices—and because two of his greatest patrons, Lucovico Sforza and Cesare Borgia, were more interested in ruling their kingdoms than in rewarding their artists. He finally attained some financial security late in life when he went to work for Louis XII and still later for Giuliano de Medici. (You have to say this for him: He couldn't have chosen four more powerful patrons.)

Toward the end of his life, while living in France, Leonardo suffered a stroke, which left his right side paralyzed. He lost the use of his right hand—but since he was left-handed, he was still able to do some final sketches before the end came at an old (for that time) sixty-seven.

Has there ever been a man of comparable talents? No. Has there ever been a man skilled in so many fields? The only name that comes to mind is Theodore Roosevelt—U.S. president, cowboy, police commissioner, war hero, best-selling author, ornithologist, explorer, big-game hunter, naturalist—but Roosevelt, for all his many accomplishments, never created anything that will live across the centuries the way Leonardo's art has done.

I persist in thinking Leonardo's greatest accomplishment wasn't his art but himself. He lived in a time when it was possible to know almost everything there was to know—and he came closer to knowing it all than any other man who ever lived.

A Timeline of Da Vinci's Life

April 15, 1452   Leonardo da Vinci is born in Anchian, near Vinci, in Tuscany.

1469   Leonardo goes to work as an apprentice of Verrocchio.

1472   Leonardo is admitted to the Guild of St. Luke, the association of Florentine painters. He assists with Verrocchio's *Baptism of Christ* and *The Annunciation*.

1475   Leonardo collaborates with Verrocchio on *Madonna with the Carnation*.

June 7, 1476   Leonardo, along with all of Verrochio's other pupils, is accused of homosexuality. The charge is later dismissed.

1478   Leonardo completes *The Annunciation*, begun in 1476.

1480   Leonardo completes *St. Jerome*.

1481   Leonardo receives a commission from the Monastery of Saint Donato a Scopeto for the *Adoration of the Magi*.

1482   Leonardo moves to Milan to work for a powerful patron, Ludovico Sforza, later to become Duke of Milan. He fails to finish his *Adoration of the Magi*.

1483   Leonardo begins work on *The Virgin of the Rocks*. (He finishes it in 1486.)

1484–1489   Along with his painting, Leonardo works on architecture and creates plans for war machines and flying machines.

1487   Leonardo begins his work on anatomy.

1490   Leonardo paints *Lady with an Ermine*.

1493   Leonardo completes a clay model of "The Great Horse" for Ludovico Sforza.

1496   Leonardo paints *The Last Supper*.

1499   Leonardo flees from Milan after the French invasion.

1500   Leonardo goes to Venice and then to Florence.

1502   Leonardo is hired by Cesare Borgia as a military engineer.

1503   Leonardo begins work on the *Mona Lisa*, and accepts a commission to paint The Battle of Anghiari.

1504   Leonardo paints *Leda and the Swan*.

1506   Leonardo returns to Milan at the invitation of the French king Louis XII and paints *The Virgin of the Rocks*.

1508   Leonardo begins work on *St. Anne,* which he finishes in 1509.

1509   Leonardo draws maps and geological surveys of Lombardy and Lake Isea and begins work on *St. John the Baptist.*

1512   Leonardo draws his *Self-Portrait.*

1513   Leonardo leaves Milan, goes to Rome to work for Giuliano de Medici. Finishes painting *St. John the Baptist.*

1516   Leonardo moves to France. His right hand is partially paralyzed by a stroke, but because he is left-handed he can still paint.

May 2, 1519   Leonardo dies near Amboise, France, and is buried in the Church of St. Florentine. His remains are later scattered during the Wars of Religion.

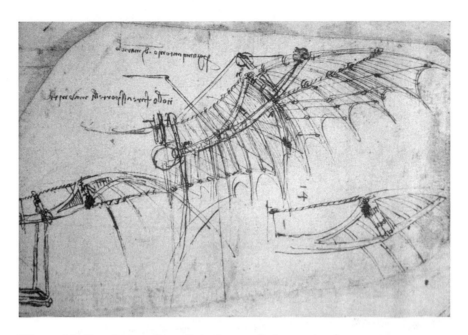

Wing with Continuous Covering. Leonardo knew that boomerangs
worked. This was an attempt to apply that same principle to something *big*.

opposite: *Mona Lisa.* This is Leonardo's masterpiece,
the most famous painting in the history of the world.
She possesses an enigmatic smile.

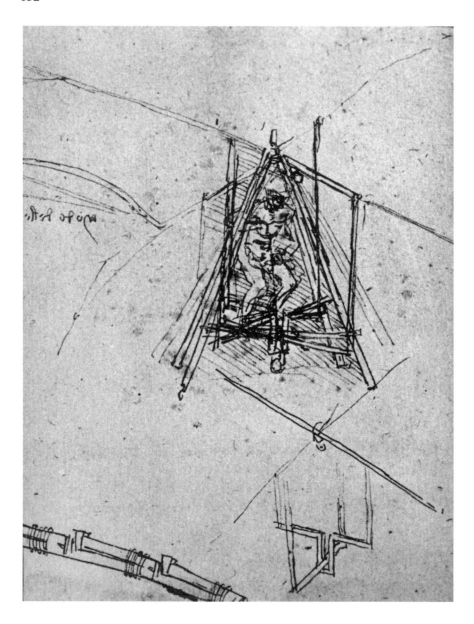

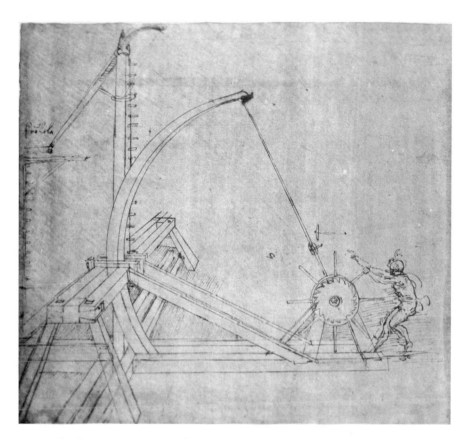

Catapult, from a page in *Codex Atlanticus*. The *Codex* contains Leonardo's
scientific drawings—the same ones he showed Mario in *Lady with an
Alien*—and this is one of the engines of war that he conceived for the
Duke of Milan.

opposite: Man in an Ornothopter.
Leonardo knew men would one day fly
and never gave up trying to devise methods
that would work.

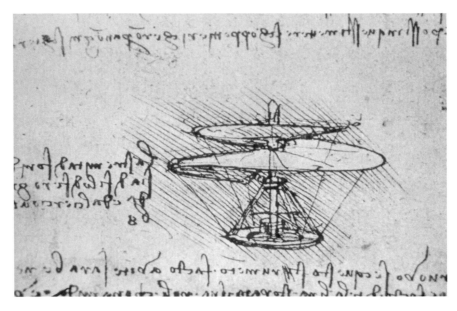

Flying Machine, sketch from *Codex Atlanticus*. Another of Leonardo's attempts to create an airplane.

FOR MORE INFORMATION

Leonardo is one of the half dozen most famous men who ever lived, so naturally there is an enormous amount of material available. I will confine myself to those books that are currently in print and easily available.

Biographies

Leonardo: The Artist and the Man, by Serge Bramly (New York: Penguin Books, 1994). Probably the most comprehensive biography.

Leonardo da Vinci, by Sherwin B. Nuland (New York: Lipper/Viking, 2000).

Art books

Leonardo da Vinci: The Complete Paintings, by Pietro C. Marani (New York: Harry N. Abrams, Inc., 2000). The most comprehensive collection of Leonardo's work.

Leonardo da Vinci: The Mind of the Renaissance, by Alessandro Vezzosi (New York: Harry N. Abrams, Inc., 1997). A more than adequate introduction to Leonardo's artwork.

Leonardo da Vinci, by D. M. Field (New York: Barnes & Noble, 2002). A very useful book, containing most of the paintings and quite a few pages from the notebooks.

Studies

The Notebooks of Leonardo da Vinci, edited by Edward MacCurdy. (Old Saybrook, CT: Konecky & Konecky). No sketches, but hundreds of pages of Leonardo's notebooks translated into English.

Math and the Mona Lisa, by Bulent Atalay (New York: Smithsonian Books, 2004). An in-depth study of Leonardo's painting methodology.

Leonardo da Vinci and a Memory of His Childhood, by Sigmund Freud (New York: Barnes & Noble, 2000; originally published in 1910).

The Paintings

Most of Leonardo's paintings are in Europe, though many travel the world on exhibit from time to time. *Lady with an Ermine* hangs in the Czartoryski Museum in Cracow, Poland. The *Mona Lisa* can be found in the Louvre in Paris. There are two versions of *The Virgin of the Rocks*, one in the Louvre, and one in London's National Gallery. *The Last Supper* can be found in Milan, at the Santa Maria delle Grazie.

The Internet

A search for Leonardo will turn up literally thousands of entries, some more trustworthy than others. These sites provide a way to see his paintings.

Look for the teacher's guide to *Lady with an Alien* at www.wgpub.com.

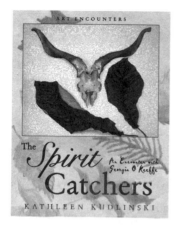

The Spirit Catchers:
An Encounter with Georgia O'Keeffe
by Kathleen Kudlinski

Like thousands of other Americans during the Great Depression, Parker Ray finds himself homeless and desperate. Now all signs—from his thirst-induced hallucinations to the inhospitable force of nature, Georgia O'Keeffe—tell him that something in the desert is out to get him.

"Kudlinski evokes the extremes of desert life, from desolation to sun-baked beauty, and then depicts the environment's mesmerizing effect on her characters . . . There are enough surprises to keep the pages turning . . . The notion of 'spirit' is woven effectively into a variety of contexts . . ." —*School Library Journal*

"Kudlinski succeeds amazingly at helping her readers look, really look, at the art of Georgia O'Keeffe."—Sam Sebasta, Ph.D., College of Education, University of Washington

". . . the plot takes off partly on the strength of Kudlinski's . . . portrait of O'Keeffe."—*Kirkus Reviews*

". . . the overwhelming feeling at the end is that the reader is 'inside the art, free to comment, and encouraged to experiment.' "—The Historical Novel Society

Hardcover ISBN: 0-8230-0408-2   Price: $15.95
Paperback ISBN: 0-8230-0412-0   Price: $6.99

Smoking Mirror:
An Encounter with Paul Gauguin
by Douglas Rees

The White Wolf killed his best friend. Now Joe Sloan seeks revenge. As he navigates the unknown territory of 1891 Tahiti and its people, he finds an unlikely ally in the French artist Paul Gauguin.

A JUNIOR LIBRARY GUILD SELECTION

"An intimate peek at Gauguin's creative process and the story behind the cover painting Matamoe with just enough action and native color to entice."
—*Kirkus Reviews*

"*Like other titles in the new Art Encounters series, this weaves biographical facts about a famous artist into a compelling novel . . . .* Rees has clearly done his research, and he admirably incorporates Gauguin's work and voice into a romantic coming-of-age story that asks compelling questions about how artists create and where their lives and art intersect. An afterword and a timeline of Gauguin's life will help readers separate fact from fiction."
—*Booklist*

"A haunting, deeply affecting book."
—Brent Hartinger, author of *Geography Club* and *The Last Chance Texaco*

Hardcover ISBN: 0-8230-4863-2   Price: $15.95
Paperback ISBN: 0-8230-4864-0   Price: $6.99

Casa Azul:

An Encounter with Frida Kahlo

by Laban Carrick Hill

Maria and Victor journey in search of their mother through a Mexico City populated by godlike wrestlers—the mighty El Corazón and his nemesis El Diablo—a blind guitarist named Old Big Eyes, and a talking monkey. But a far more magical place exists: Casa Azul, the home of the painter Frida Kahlo.

". . . Hill's blend of realism, fantasy and Aztec myth nicely mirrors Kahlo's surreal juxtaposition of real and unreal in her lifelong attempt to paint her own reality. Magical realism from cover to cover." —*Kirkus Reviews*

"Like his subject's art, Laban Hill's encounter with Frida Kahlo is a richly imagined, seamless mixture of magic and reality that reveals, for readers, the larger truth of the artist's passionate life and work." —Michael Cart, editor, *Rush Hour*

"The book and the whole story are great. I felt like a kid reading every word on the page! I like the strains of magical realism coming through. The story has charm and reads like a thriller." —Margarita Aguilar, assistant curator, El Museo del Barrio

"Highly recommended to introduce the sophisticated young reader to this fascinating artist. —*Children's Literature*

Hardcover ISBN: 0-8230-4863-2   Price: $15.95

The Wedding:
An Encounter with Jan van Eyck
by Elizabeth M. Rees

In fifteenth-century Belgium, young Giovanna Cenami resists an arranged marriage in favor of true love. Who wouldn't choose a handsome and valiant youth over a seemingly dull merchant ten years her senior? Or is there more than meets the eye?

" . . . Rees, a painter herself, brings Jan van Eyck's vision to life in ways few could have imagined. Though set in 15th-century Europe, Giovanna's struggles seem both appropriate to her time and relevant to the struggles facing American teenagers."
—Rochelle Ratner, executive editor, *American Book Review*

"A page-turning, lively historical YA romance plot spiced with a soupçon of star-crossed lovers . . . . Along the way, readers will encounter well-integrated, fascinating information on the period as well as the materials and techniques of the painting."
—*Kirkus Reviews*

"A story as rich and textured as the painting that inspired it."
—Ellen Steiber, author of *A Rumor of Gems*

"Elizabeth M. Rees has a true gift for bringing art and history vividly to life. Her story kept me up until the wee hours of the night, and I didn't want to leave the 15th century when it was done!"
—Terri Windling, six-time World Fantasy award-winning author of *The Wood Wife*

Hardcover ISBN: 0-8230-0407-4   Price: $15.95